D1391872

The Most Precious Bundle of All
Tears, triumphs and a tiny miracle

An IVF mix-up turns two couple's dreams of parenthood into a nightmare.

But through the tests, tears and triumphs they find unexpected love…and realise that happy endings come in all shapes and sizes!

Fighting to keep the baby she's always wanted, Olivia turns to dashing doctor David for love and support in

HER MOTHERHOOD WISH
by Anne Fraser

Meet John and Lily. Discovering they've made a baby turns these strangers' worlds upside down—but not nearly as much as when they start falling in love!

A BOND BETWEEN STRANGERS
by Scarlet Wilson

Both titles are available now

Dear Reader

I was absolutely delighted to be asked to write a linked duet with fellow author Anne Fraser. After much brainstorming and lots of e-mails this was the story we finally agreed on.

The story is about a wrongly implanted embryo, and is told from the point of view of the father. John Carter created embryos with an egg donor for use in his marriage. But his marriage is long since over and, due to legal issues, he expects to receive a letter from the clinic telling him that his embryos have been destroyed. Instead he receives a letter telling him that his embryo was mistakenly implanted into another woman some months before!

Lily Grayson became an egg donor after learning some family history and to help fund herself through college. Having a gorgeous man accost her at an airfield and ask for help to get his baby back is the last thing she expects!

The outcomes aren't straightforward either—which gave us lots of leeway with this story. How do both couples get a happy-ever-after from a story like this?

You can let us know if you think we succeeded!

Feel free to contact me via my website: www.scarlet-wilson.com

Many thanks

Scarlet

A BOND
BETWEEEN
STRANGERS

BY
SCARLET WILSON

This book is dedicated to my two lovely sisters, Jennifer Dickson and Valerie Glencross, reliable, beautiful and devoted to their families. There's no greater gift than the gift of sisters!

First published in Great Britain 2012
by Mills & Boon, an imprint of Harlequin (UK) Limited.
Harlequin (UK) Limited, Eton House, 18-24 Paradise Road,
Richmond, Surrey TW9 1SR

© Scarlet Wilson 2012

ISBN: 978 0 263 22888 5

Harlequin (UK) policy is to use papers that are natural, renewable and recyclable products and made from wood grown in sustainable forests. The logging and manufacturing process conform to the legal environmental regulations of the country of origin.

Printed and bound in Great Britain
by CPI Antony Rowe, Chippenham, Wiltshire

Scarlet Wilson wrote her first story aged eight and has never stopped. Her family have fond memories of *Shirley and the Magic Purse*, with its army of mice, all with names beginning with the letter 'm'. An avid reader, Scarlet started with every Enid Blyton book, moved on to the *'Chalet School'* series, and many years later found Mills and Boon®.

She trained and worked as a nurse and health visitor, and now currently works in public health. For her, finding medical romances was a match made in heaven. She is delighted to find herself among the authors she has read for many years.

Scarlet lives on the West Coast of Scotland with her fiancé and their two sons.

Recent titles by the same author:

WEST WING TO MATERNITY WING!
THE BOY WHO MADE THEM LOVE AGAIN
IT STARTED WITH A PREGNANCY.

These books are also available in eBook format from www.millsandboon.co.uk

PROLOGUE

JOHN CARTER'S feet thudded along the pavement in rapid, regular beats. The early morning sun was beating down on his back, trickles of sweat pooling around the waistband of his shorts. He rounded the corner of his street, slowing to a stop outside his house.

He leaned forward, taking slow, practised breaths as his heart continued thudding against his chest. He'd been running this same route along the San Francisco Bay area for the last two years, but it didn't seem to get any easier.

He grabbed his water bottle from his waistband and took a slug. Right now he was wishing it contained anything but water. The flag on the mailbox was up. The mailman had been early today.

John took a few moments to stretch out his aching limbs. His hamstring twitched again. Damn. He'd agreed to play five-a-side soccer tonight with some English colleagues. The last thing he needed was a pulled hamstring.

He reached into the mailbox and pulled out the barrage of catalogues and envelopes. A frown creased his face and he walked up towards his porch. He sat on the decking outside as he sorted through the mail, glancing at his watch. In another fifteen minutes' time he'd have had a quick shower and be at work, ready to spend most of the day in the operating theatre. There wasn't even any point going into the kitchen. The fridge was virtually empty and so were his cupboards. He'd discovered as much when he'd got home late last night, starving after spending hours in the office. He didn't even have any coffee left. No matter how much he tried to avoid it, he was really going to have to do a grocery shop some time soon.

He flicked past the usual array of catalogues containing clothes, make-up, candles, jewellery—or the latest 'diet' miracle—all addressed to his ex-wife, Tabitha Carter.

Without blinking an eye, he tossed them all into his nearby rubbish bin. It wasn't as if she'd come looking for them. Wherever Tabitha had ended up, doubtless she'd re-sent for them all. Two years on, many tears and tantrums later, his divorce attorney still hadn't tracked the woman down—though thankfully he had managed to acquire her signature.

The only thing she wanted from him these days were the alimony cheques.

His fingers stopped their automatic trawl through the mail. The usual bills and free offers were ignored. One envelope was different from the rest. Bulkier. Heavier-quality paper, premium bonded. And although there was no emblem, he'd recognise their mail anywhere.

This was it. The final nail in the coffin of his disastrous marriage.

He sighed and looked out over the family-friendly cul-de-sac where they'd lived. Tabitha had never fitted in here. She'd hated the fact that everyone's kids played out in the front yards. She'd hated little people trooping

in and out of their home in a search for cookies or someone to fix their bikes.

This was the perfect family home.

Just not for them.

The initial fertility tests had created more toddler-
sized tantrums than he'd ever seen. The discovery that
Tabitha didn't have any viable eggs had taken her months
to recover from. The selection of an egg donor had almost resulted in their first major fallout. The first round
of IVF had been fraught with difficulties—mainly because Tabitha hadn't followed any of the instructions
she'd been given.

The second round of IVF had resulted in an ectopic
pregnancy. At this point Tabitha had refused to tolerate
any more treatment.

And by this stage John had been inclined to agree.
The cracks in their marriage had migrated into a fully
fledged San Andreas fault.

Tabitha's leaving hadn't really had an impact on him.
Emptying the joint bank account and driving off in his
new car hadn't created more than a few minor inconve-
niences. It had also gave him free rein to buy the Ducati
motorbike he'd really wanted.

He'd just been happy she'd left the house intact.

But the thought of never having kids, never having
the family that he'd always wanted, cut him deeper than
he could ever have imagined.

There was still time. He still had some chance of
meeting someone new, someone who might want to settle down and have kids. But at his age, thirty-nine, the
chances seemed to be reducing every day. It had been
three years since they'd tried IVF—two years since
Tabitha had left. And in two years? He hadn't had one
date that had remotely interested him. Too young, too

old. Too career orientated, and the best one—the women who were only interested in him because he was a doctor.

Just like Tabitha. Once bitten, twice shy.

He turned the letter over in his hands.

This was it. His final dealings with the clinic. The letter telling him that the remaining viable embryos had been destroyed.

And for now his hopes of fatherhood would have to be put to one side.

He tore open the envelope, pulled out the letter and scanned the page.

He gave a jolt. As if a bolt of electricity had just ran through his body. He stood up, his body on autopilot, his eyes never leaving the page as he tried to take in the words. '...our sincerest apologies...never in our clinic's history...wrongly implanted...numerous messages.'

He marched into his house. Sure enough. The answering-machine was blinking. He hadn't looked at it in the last three days—work had been crazy. Sixteen messages. He didn't even need to listen to them. He started stripping off his running gear as he strode into the shower. Work was the last place he would be today.

Somewhere out there—someone was carrying his baby.

CHAPTER ONE

LILY GRAYSON carried out her safety checks one last time. It didn't matter that she was jumping with a fully qualified instructor. It didn't matter that this airfield and accompanying flying school had an impeccable record. It didn't matter that a fully qualified rigger would have already packed her chute. It didn't matter that she was almost fully qualified herself.

Lily always checked her own parachutes—main and reserve—herself. Period. For an adrenaline junkie like Lily it was all part of the build up to the event. Part of the rush.

She gave a little smile as she glanced down at her new bright purple flight suit, complete with pink writing on the back, 'Here Comes Lily'. No one could miss her.

She was fed up with wearing the ugly khaki regulation suits. This was her third jump for charity—her twentieth for herself—so she'd decided the investment was worth it. She pulled on her matching helmet and wandered over to where the newbies stood. They were hanging onto instructor Ryan's every word as if their lives depended on it—which, in fact, it probably did. Their knees were trembling so much the sound was almost audible.

She couldn't remember ever feeling like that. Why be scared? This was one of the most exhilarating things in the world. The feeling when you jumped out into nothing, the smack of the air hitting your cheeks, streaming through the tiny hairs sticking out the back of your helmet. The whoosh when you pulled the cord and you were suspended in mid-air and the ground was rushing up to meet you.

The palms of her hands itched. She couldn't wait to get up there.

'Hi, stranger. You again. What charity did you hoodwink this time to get a free jump?'

Dan, one of the other jump instructors, flung an easy arm around her shoulders. His six-foot-five frame dwarfed her five feet five.

She shot him a grin. 'I'll have you know I'm about to raise over seven thousand dollars for a leading children's cancer charity. They were very keen when I offered to jump for them.' A glint appeared in her eye. This was definitely a two-way street. She got to do the thing she loved and the cancer charity got to make money. She wished she'd thought of this years ago.

'I just need another five minutes with these guys.' Dan waved his arm towards the nervous participants.

Lily gave a nod. The hangar was hot today and she unbuttoned the top of the flight suit and wriggled her arms out, tying it at her waist. The bright pink T-shirt she wore matched the writing on her suit and the jump shoes on her feet. She wandered over to the open hangar doors and stood looking out over the airfield.

There were several planes being prepared and she gave a smile as one of the pilots gave her a wave. That was what she liked about this place. All friends. No drama. Just a warm welcome whenever you arrived.

Out of the corner of her eye she caught sight of a motorbike speeding along the country road. He was going far too fast. But, then, he was obviously experienced, hugging the corners and dipping down towards the road.

She saw his helmet rise as if looking for the turn-off then, sure enough, he signalled and moved into the airfield. She shook her head. She'd no idea who he was, but there was no way Dan would let anyone jump without the full briefing. Evel Knievel would have to wait for the next jump.

Carter felt his heart pounding in his chest. Almost two weeks on and his world had collapsed around him. His wayward ex-wife couldn't be found.

He'd spent exorbitant amounts of money hiring an attorney and a private detective. The attorney was dealing with all the legal aspects from the clinic as Carter was too angry to speak to them right now. The private detective? So far, he'd been to Los Angeles and Las Vegas and found nothing.

Not even his ex-wife's bank would help. They wouldn't even tell him how she was accessing his money.

His attorney was an old friend from college and had made a new suggestion. It was probably for the best that Tabitha couldn't be found—she would be horrified by what had happened, and she probably wasn't a poster girl for motherhood.

But Carter and Tabitha had spent a long time selecting their egg donor from the hundreds of women on file with the clinic. He'd seen her picture, knew what age she was, knew she had an Ivy League education and knew she lived locally. How hard could it be to find her?

And so he'd put his private detective to work again. To track down his egg donor. And he'd found her. Lily Grayson, twenty-seven. Trained at University of Pennsylvania and working as a nurse in one of the other

San Francisco hospitals. And today she was here, doing a jump for one of the charities.

He swung his leg over the bike and stretched his back, pulling off his helmet and looking around him. How hard could she be to find? He'd been here before. He'd done a few jumps from here—another of his thrill factors. Maybe he'd find someone who knew her?

He could see a number of figures around one of the hangars and moved swiftly in that direction. A woman was leaning against the hangar door, her bright purple flight suit around her waist, her pink helmet in her hand.

He glanced quickly at his photo. No, she was definitely a blonde. The woman he was looking for was a brunette. Pity.

She sat her helmet at her feet and folded her arms across her chest, covering his view of her well-shaped body. 'Well, lucky me,' came the sassy voice as she raised her eyes skyward. 'Someone up there has definitely been listening to my requests. A big, solid, dark-haired leather-clad biker, all to myself.'

He could see the smile dancing around her lips. And he could smell her perfume, but it wasn't spicy like her, it was light and floral, a scent he recognised from his garden—honeysuckle.

'And who might you be looking for?' she continued. There was a twinkle in her brown eyes and for a second he almost wished they were green. Like the photo in his pocket.

It was the first time in a long time he'd felt inclined to flirt.

He sighed, then gave her a smile anyway. 'I'm looking for a beautiful woman, but unfortunately she's a brunette, not a blonde.' He gave a nod at her blonde hair.

'Damn! I thought blondes were meant to have more fun?'

Curiosity piqued him. 'What's your name?'

'Now, why would I tell my name to a man who prefers brunettes?' She was as sharp as a whip. 'What's your name, stranger?'

He liked her. For the first time in a long time he actually liked a woman. 'John Carter. But my friends just call me Carter.'

'Then I guess I should just call you John.' Her answer came as quick as a flash. She stuck her hand out towards him and looked over her shoulder. 'Here, at this airfield, they call me Dynamo.'

Their hands met, the electricity between them so loud it practically crackled. She was slim without being skinny, but with enough curves to make you look twice.

Carter gave a wider smile, 'I wonder why....' His voice trailed off then he fixed his eyes on her again. 'Dynamo seems appropriate.'

She looked over to the car park. 'How long have you had your bike?'

He shrugged. 'A couple of years. I'd wanted one for quite a while and when the opportunity arose, I grabbed it with both hands.' He looked back at his bike. 'Probably time to trade it in for a newer version.'

Her brow puckered. 'I like the colour scheme. It's even nicer than my baby.' She pointed to the other end of the car park where her silver and red Ducati was parked.

He gave a little start of surprise. 'Looks like we're a matching pair.' His eyes met hers.

She looked up and down his tall frame. 'Most of the bikers I meet in San Francisco are the long-haired, hairy type. Either that or they're gay. Where did you spring from?'

He snorted with laughter. Her sassy attitude and spark was beginning to draw him in. Make him lose focus and forget the reason he was there. To find the donor. To win back his child.

He straightened his shoulders. 'Nice to meet you, Dynamo, but I'd better be going.' He strode off into the hangar.

'Hey, John,' she shouted after him, pausing whilst he turned back round. 'I think you should reconsider your decision. You're cutting out almost half of the female population, restricting yourself to brunettes.' A twinkle appeared in her eyes, 'Plus you didn't ask if I was a natural blonde.' And with that she stuck her helmet back on her head and headed out onto the airstrip.

He gave her a smile, holding back his laughter at the pointed use of his first name. Who on earth was she? He walked further into the hangar to the group of nervous-looking jumpers, all standing in their regulation flight suits next to their carefully packed parachutes. 'Hey, Dan, I was wondering if you could help me find someone?' Dan was leaning downwards, looking at someone's ankle, and Carter gave him a slap on the shoulder.

Dan didn't miss a beat. 'Perfect. Carter, take a look at this for me. This man's been bothered with his ankle this week and developed a limp—I don't think it's wise for him to jump at the moment.'

Carter fell to his knees and stripped the ankle of the thick woollen sock protecting it. The dark purple bruises made him sit back. He gave a wry smile, 'I don't even need to touch that.' He shook his head. 'There's no way you can jump with an ankle like that. Your ankles take all the impact when you land. You could do some serious damage.'

The man looked panicked. 'But I'm about to raise three thousand dollars for the charity. If I don't do it, the charity won't get the money.'

Dan looked from one to the other. 'Does it have to be you that does the jump or does it just have to be someone?'

The man blinked. 'Eh....someone, I think.' He held his hands up. 'But there's no extra people around and we're due to take off in ten minutes. Where on earth will you find a replacement?'

Dan's face broke into a wild smile. 'Easiest thing in the world. Meet Carter. High-flying doc. Done more jumps than I could count. I'm sure he'll fill in for you—won't you, Carter?'

Carter hesitated—obviously for a fraction too long because Dan slid an arm around his shoulders. 'It's for charity.' He tapped him on the chest. 'And I know you, you wouldn't want the charity to lose money because they didn't have enough people to do their jump.'

Carter sighed. 'I'll do it on one condition.'

Dan raised his eyebrows, 'And what's that?'

'You help me find this girl—Lily Grayson. Someone at the hospital where she works told me she was doing a jump here today.' He'd pulled the crumpled photograph from his pocket. It was already looking dog-eared. He'd printed it from his computer off the clinic's website.

Dan's eyes narrowed. 'Why are you looking for Lily? Has she done something wrong?' Almost immediately Carter sensed the vibe. The protective vibe. He'd be wise not to say too much if he was looking for help.

'No—nothing's wrong. She's done something really good. I just wanted to thank her.' Not strictly true, but it was the best he could do at short notice.

Dan looked over Carter's leather-clad figure. 'Better get changed, then. Lily's up in the next jump—you can thank her then.' He pointed in the direction of the lockers, 'Take one of my suits, they'll fit you fine. But be quick, we need to be ready to go in five minutes.'

Carter strode over to the lockers, stripping off his leather jacket and unfastening his trousers. He found alternative clothes in Dan's locker and pulled them on before donning the red flight suit and matching helmet. He glanced back around the room. There were several women there. But all had their helmets hiding their hair and faces. Hopefully Dan would point Lily out once they got in the plane.

He spent the next few minutes checking his parachute and signing his paperwork. Since he'd done it so many times before it was all routine to him. He caught sight of the purple-suited figure scrambling onto the plane ahead of him. What was that writing on her back?

He moved through the crowd until he was closer to Dan. 'Which one's Lily?' he asked as they stepped into the aircraft.

The rest of the party was all sitting along the sides of the plane, ready for take-off. Dan looked up. 'Far end. Purple flight suit, pink helmet. This is her twentieth jump.'

The engine and propeller started up, filling the back of the aircraft with noise. Carter felt a lump in his throat. She was Lily?

The one woman he'd met in the past year that he'd had even the vaguest connection with? It seemed unreal.

Worse than that, it was a disaster. She was as much a daredevil as he was. Twenty jumps? She'd almost matched his record. Plus, a matching Ducati.

He groaned. This wasn't what he'd hoped for. Worse than that, this wasn't what his attorney had hoped for.

When they hadn't been able to find Tabitha, the attorney had suggested trying another tactic. They needed to build a case for Carter to keep the baby that some other woman was currently carrying.

The genetics might be obvious. But some judges took pity on the poor woman implanted with the wrong baby and the possible risks to her health. This woman wasn't a willing surrogate. This woman had thought she was getting a baby of her own.

In a way, it was lucky they'd only found out at around the twenty-eight-week mark. By that point she had been visibly pregnant and it had been too late for termination—no matter what the reason.

Carter needed to build a case for himself. He needed to prove he could be an able parent. And with no current partner, that could be difficult. Sometimes judges, rightly or wrongly, didn't look favourably on male, single parents. So his attorney had suggested he find the egg donor.

It shouldn't be too hard—he'd already seen her photograph and knew her most basic details via the clinic database. But he only had a few days to do it. The newspapers had already got a whiff of the story and any day now it was going to be front-page news. So he had to find her quickly. All he had to do was persuade her to side with him in court. Maybe even pretend to have a vested interest in this baby.

What sort of woman would give up their eggs? What woman would choose to be an egg donor? There had to be a good reason for it and Carter hoped he could find it.

He glanced down the plane towards Lily. Now he understood the comment about 'being a natural blonde'— she wasn't. But that didn't explain her eye colour. In the clinic photograph her eyes were green. But today they were definitely brown.

Something twisted inside his gut. Could she have lied about something like that? Her eye colour had been one of the reasons that they'd picked her—that, and her Ivy League education. Eye colour had been important because Tabitha had green eyes too so it meant a closer match to them.

Carter felt the plane beginning to circle. Dan stood up and walked along the plane, giving everyone a number. The first-timers were going to go first. Some of them were tandem-jumping with an instructor, so Carter edged up the bench out of their way.

He found himself next to Lily and she unsuspectingly gave him another wide grin. 'I didn't know you were a fellow jumper.' She smiled. 'I thought you came to find a woman.'

'I did.' He looked at her closely. Was she wearing contacts? Brown ones?

Lily shifted uncomfortably under his gaze. This lighthearted flirtation suddenly felt different. Maybe it was being stuck in the back of a plane with a virtual stranger who was looking at her oddly. But something about this was making her uneasy.

She bit her lip. 'Then who is she?'

Carter fumbled in his pocket and pulled out the rumpled photograph. 'She's Lily Grayson.' He pushed her shoulders forward a little to read the writing across her back. '"Here Comes Lily"—I take it that means you.'

Lily took the photograph from his hands, staring at the person on the paper. She recognised the photograph immediately and knew exactly where it had come from. In the photograph she looked different, her hair was brown with curls. 'That seems like years ago,' she murmured.

'More than three years, to be precise.'

She jerked at the edge to his words. He was sitting so close to her. It was hard to hear in the back of the aircraft and his lips were brushing her ear. Nothing about this felt right.

Her stomach started to churn. This had to be about egg donation. It was the only place she'd used that photograph. Was something wrong? Had a baby been born with some horrible disease from an egg she'd donated?

'What's with the eye colour?' he asked.

She frowned. 'What do you mean?'

'In your profile you said you had green eyes. But today…' he leaned right in so their noses were almost touching '…your eyes are definitely brown.'

She drew backwards and wrinkled her nose, shaking her head. 'Who are you—the eye-colour police?' She shrugged her shoulders. 'I didn't think the green eyes went well with my new blonde look, so I changed them.'

She looked at his stunned face. 'What? You haven't heard of coloured contacts? Or, did you think I'd lied in my clinic application?'

She stared at his serious face and leaned backwards. All of this was making her uncomfortable. As far as she knew, she didn't have any genetic disorder than would cause problems for a baby. So why on earth would he be looking for her? And more importantly, why did he have to be so darned handsome? 'What exactly do you want, Mr Carter?'

'I'm looking for someone to help me.'

'Help you do what?'

'I want you to help me get my baby back.'

CHAPTER TWO

THIS couldn't be happening. Lily's stomach lurched. Here she was, stuck in the back of an aircraft, with some nut. The only way out was to jump, and right now they were nowhere near the landing zone. She couldn't have made this up.

She tried to edge along the bench a little, away from crazy John Carter. All of a sudden the flirtation was lost. She didn't want to swap jibes with him any more. She wanted to get as far away as possible.

The aircraft started to circle—maybe they were closer to the landing zone than she'd thought—and one of the instructors pulled open the side door, shouting instructions to the petrified jumpers.

The air swept through the cabin, taking whatever words John was trying to shout in her direction with it. She shook her head and tapped the side of her helmet, hoping he would understand.

This would give her some time. Some time to plan a way to get away from him. Her eyes shot over to Dan, hoping he would see the panic on her face and help her out. But he gave her a huge grin, obviously thinking the flirtation between them was continuing. He walked down the plane, repeating everyone's number.

Seven. She was number seven. Carter was number nine. She could lose him in the sky.

She jerked as some fingers squeezed hers. 'We need to talk,' he mouthed at her, then pointed downwards. 'On the ground.'

She nodded wordlessly. As soon as her feet touched the ground she intended to grab the first vehicle back to the airfield and leave as quickly as possible on her Ducati. She would leave her clothes in her locker.

Her mind churned. What kind of idiot came looking for an egg donor? Wasn't she supposed to be left alone?

She'd had reservations about putting her photo and details on the clinic's private website, but she'd been assured that only clients who had passed all the psychological tests would be given access to the site. Only people who were preparing for treatment and needed to select a genetically compatible donor.

Plus the fact no other clinic had paid the same benefits as the San Francisco clinic. She'd managed to wipe out most of her college debts by donating eggs on three occasions. Ivy League colleges like University of Pennsylvania didn't come cheap. And egg donation had seemed like a simple and humanitarian way to fund it.

And it wasn't like she was the only one. Seven of the nursing students in her class had all been on the clinic's database. Clients loved Ivy League women. They paid top dollar for them.

Lily cringed at the memory. It had been more than three years since her last egg donation. It had seemed so easy at the time. Help some couple to have the child they'd always wanted and pay off her college debts, with no lasting damage to herself. She was young and healthy. She wasn't in a permanent relationship and wasn't planning kids in the near future. There was also that tiny mat-

ter of early menopause that ran in her family. This gave
her an added security blanket. Eggs stored for future
use by her, if she needed them. What could go wrong?

John Carter could go wrong.

Surely there was something in the clinic protocols
that said he wasn't allowed to contact her? She'd check
when she got home.

From the corner of her eye she saw Dan signalling
her. She stood up and took her position in the queue at
the door. Number five seemed to be stalling. Seemed
to be having second thoughts. Dan leaned forward and
spoke a few words of encouragement in their ear, urging them on.

Lily held her breath. If number five didn't hurry up
she would be tempted to give him an almighty shove. She
was conscious of Carter standing almost behind her. She
was sure she could feel his breath at the back of her neck.

If it had been any other circumstances, it might have
felt quite sexy. Flirting with a tall, dark, handsome
stranger and then jumping out an aircraft with him. But
right now all Lily wanted to do was get as far away from
John Carter as possible.

Carter chewed on his bottom lip. This wasn't going quite
as planned.

Maybe his attorney was wrong. Maybe this wasn't
a good idea. It didn't help that for a few mad seconds
they'd actually flirted with each other. He'd never have
done that if he'd realised she was Lily Grayson.

A smile danced across his lips. That might not strictly
be true. Lily was the first smart-mouthed girl he'd met
in a long time. The first woman he'd felt even the slightest bit of interest in.

Maybe now hadn't been the best time to tell her that

he was looking for her. But he didn't like lies. He didn't like deceit.

She shifted in front of him and he took a sharp intake of breath. She was uncomfortable. Did she think he was some kind of madman? Stalking her from a clinic website?

He couldn't wait to get back on firm ground. He couldn't wait to sit down and talk to her calmly, rationally and in an environment where they could actually hear each other.

They shuffled forward as the nervous number five finally made his jump. Ahead of them number six stepped out as if he jumped from a plane every day. And Lily was right behind him, the bright purple suit disappearing into oblivion before his eyes.

He felt his heart lurch. He didn't want to lose her on the way down. He'd done enough of these jumps to know that not everyone landed in the spot they should.

He bit his lip impatiently as number eight took a few seconds to speak to Dan on the way out. Hurry up!

Finally, the doorway was clear. He gave Dan a salute on the way past and stepped out into nothing.

Perfection.

The air streamed up all around him and he spread his arms and legs wide in the cold air. Beneath him he could see the other jumpers. Lily's purple suit wasn't difficult to spot. She was underneath him and a little to his left.

Carter pulled his legs and arms in, streamlining his body and pointing downwards in her direction. The least he could do was catch her up.

Lily was finally back in her comfort zone. Adrenaline pumped through her body, her arms and legs spread wide, and she was flying.

The cold air buffeted her cheeks and swept through

the tiny strands of hair poking out from her helmet. This was freedom. This was space. This was clean air.

Two out of three things that San Francisco sometimes lacked.

She could see one of the jumpers pulling their chute as she streamed past. If her face could have drawn a frown it would have. It was far too early.

She closed her eyes for a second. Plenty of time to pull her parachute. A shadow passed in front of her and she opened her eyes to see John Carter, in his borrowed, bright red flight suit coasting next to her. How on earth had he caught up with her?

All of a sudden the space, clear air and freedom seemed to shrink around her. He was ruining everything!

He signalled to her, giving her a thumbs-up and a wide grin. Right now she could happily stick her thumb right in his eye.

She changed position. He was too close, and he should know that. Pulling ripcords right now could result in their lines getting tangled—the last thing any jumper wanted.

She took a deep breath, deciding she'd moved far enough away from him, and pulled the cord. A sharp tug pulled her upwards as the brightly coloured rectangular parachute released above her, slowing her descent. She looked downwards towards the ground. Normally she would have waited a little longer to pull, but John Carter had annoyed her, he'd ruined the jump for her anyway, so what difference did it make when she pulled her cord?

She adjusted her steering toggles to move herself towards the landing area. Her heart was still hammering against her chest and she couldn't quite work out whether it was the effect of the jump or the effect of John Carter.

She twisted her head from side to side. Where had he

gone? She heard a shout to her right, and turned again. There he was in the sky, just above her. Anger lit a fire in her belly. What on earth did he want with her? Why wouldn't he just leave her alone?

Her normal, solid concentration was rocked and she heard another shout above her. Too late, she realised she hadn't slowed her descent enough to land. She pulled sharply on both her steering toggles, trying to brake, but with little effect as she thudded to the ground. A sharp pain tore up her right calf.

Seconds later there was a soft thud beside her and a flash of red. John Carter appeared in front of her, kneeling on the ground and starting to examine her leg. Even the lightest touch was painful. 'Ow!' she yelped, pulling her ankle backwards. 'What do you think you're doing?'

His voice was calm and steady. 'Examining your leg.' He loosened the laces on her boot and gently slid it from her foot. He leaned forward and pressed the release button for her parachute, which was currently buffeting in the wind and tugging at her shoulders.

'Let go of me!' Lily shouted, fury building inside her. 'This is entirely your fault anyway. If you hadn't distracted me when I was landing, this would never have happened.'

Carter stopped for a second and looked thoughtful. Then he held his hand out towards her. 'We've not been properly introduced and that's my fault. John Carter, Orthopaedist at San Francisco General.'

She stopped and caught her breath, then wriggled her ankle experimentally. It still hurt. Did she really want to alienate the one person in this field who could probably help her? Her hand reached out and touched his. There it was again. The spark she'd felt earlier in the hangar. That weird little zing that appeared out of thin air.

She stared at his hand. Tanned skin, blunt, straight-cut fingernails. It was a firm, strong handshake. His large hand dwarfed her small one. But it was the sensations around it that were concerning her.

He gave a wry smile as he touched her ankle again, peeling down her sock and touching her bare skin just above the ankle. 'I think you might be in need of my services.'

In more ways than one. Lily's face paled and she pulled her head back to reality. 'You're joking, right? It's a sprain or a bruise, isn't it?'

Carter shook his head. 'Can't say for sure until I've seen an X-ray, but I'm almost sure you've fractured your tibia—just above your ankle. It's pretty common for people involved in extreme sports.'

Lily raised her eyebrow at him. 'Extreme sports? Does this qualify? I would have thought doing a charity jump for a children's cancer charity was anything but extreme.'

She grimaced as he rolled her thick sock down over her ankle. Almost before her eyes her ankle started to swell. If she hadn't seen it for herself, she wouldn't have believed it.

His fingers were light, delicate with their touch, realising how sensitive the area must be. There wasn't any other reason her skin tingled under his touch. 'Can't you just strap it? It's not sore enough to be broken.' As if to prove her point, Lily pulled herself to her feet and attempted to bear her weight. 'There,' she said, her lips tightly pressed together, as she pushed her foot on the ground. 'It'll be fine once I get some strapping on it.'

Carter walked around her other side and slid his arm around her waist, taking some of her weight. 'There's no way that ankle is fine. I'd bet my career on it.'

Dan appeared next to them, a mound of colourful

parachute in his arms. 'Did you hurt yourself, Lily? Is something up?'

She wrinkled her nose. 'Bad landing. Somebody distracted me at the last minute. But I'm sure it's just a sprain.'

Dan shook his head. 'The doc doesn't get these things wrong. Better go back to his place and get it seen to.' He tossed a set of keys to Carter. 'Take the pick-up. I won't need it for a few hours.' He pointed across the field. 'I've got parachutes to repack.'

'His place!' Lily exploded. 'I don't think so!'

Carter smirked, his arm tightening around her waist. He looked down at the fiery bundle in his arms. 'I think he meant it figuratively. He didn't mean my house—he meant San Francisco General.' He stopped for a second then gave her a wicked glance. 'But I can take you back to my place if that's what you want.'

Lily mumbled under her breath. That was the last thing she wanted. She was trying to get away from John Carter. Not end up indebted to him.

His arm swept underneath her, catching her beneath the knees and cradling her between his arms.

'What on earth do you think you're doing?'

'My job,' he muttered as he took long strides towards the pick-up a few hundred yards away. 'Best keep the weight off that.'

Lily fumbled in the pocket of her flight suit, pulling out her smartphone. 'If you let me know where we're going, I can text one of my friends to meet us there.'

'Uh-huh.' John Carter made the right noises, but shook his head as he swung open the pick-up's door and plunked her down on the passenger seat.

'What does that mean—uh-huh? Is that yes or no?'

'Don't you ever stop talking?' Carter slid in the driver's door next to her and clicked his seat belt in place. He folded his arms across his chest. 'I'm taking you to the ER at San Francisco General. I'll be able to fast-track you through and get you X-rayed. Once I've seen those X-rays we'll discuss what type of treatment you need.' He pointed at her phone, 'And put that away. There's no point calling in anyone until we know what's happening. And anyway we need some privacy—we need to talk.'

'Talk about what, exactly?' Lily's voice rose in pitch. She was getting more stressed by the second. She was being kidnapped by a gorgeous, slightly crazy doctor. Was this one of her mad dreams? Any minute now she'd look down and she'd be wearing a princess dress.

Carter started the pick-up and moved off, concentrating on the rugged terrain of the field and its effects on his passenger. He kept his mouth closed. The last thing he needed to do right now was upset Lily. He needed her on his side if he'd any chance at all of getting his baby back.

Had she felt it too? He thought he'd seen something flash in her eyes when he'd touched her. That connection. That crazy feeling of something happening.

He shot her a sideways glance. She looked totally different from the photo on file at the clinic. If they'd lined up a dozen women, he would never have picked out Lily as the woman in the photo.

She caught him staring. 'What is it? What are you looking at?'

His eyes ran over her body. 'You're not exactly what I was expecting.'

'What's that supposed to mean?'

Carter frowned. 'You don't look anything like your picture.'

Lily wrinkled her nose. 'Are you talking about the hair?' she lifted her hand self-consciously to touch her

dyed blonde locks. 'Funny thing about donor clinics—
they're not big on any type of toxin being introduced
into the body—including hair dye. So, while I was on the
books, so to speak, I had to stick to my natural colour.'

Carter nodded slowly. Lily was going to prove tougher
work than his attorney had thought. 'So you're not on
the books now?'

She shook her head. 'I shouldn't be. I thought my profile had been taken down. Why? Did you find it there?'

Carter pulled off the field onto the smooth tarmac.
The hospital was only a fifteen-minute journey away.
Fifteen minutes to try and persuade Lily Grayson to help
him win his baby back.

Lily's eyes were fixed on the road ahead. 'To be perfectly honest, I'm a bit freaked out by all this. Last time I
donated my eggs was over three years ago. The last thing
I expected was someone to turn up and ask me questions about it.' She shifted around in her seat so she was
facing him. 'What exactly do you want, John Carter?'

Carter shifted in his seat. In an ideal world he would
have tracked Lily Grayson down, knocked on her door
and sat down and spoke about this rationally, convinc-
ing her to help him out.

But in the last two weeks things had exploded around
him. His ex-wife had vanished without a trace. The letter from the clinic had just been the tip of the iceberg.
His life had been transformed into a whirlwind of frantic telephone calls, internet searches and visits to his attorney. He'd barely had the chance to really think about
what all this meant. There were so many legal complications. So many things he could never have considered.

Asking Lily Grayson for help was one of them.

How fair was it that he had to ask a virtual stranger
for help to get his baby back?

He swerved the truck, pulling into the side of the road and turning to face Lily. 'I'm sorry about this, Lily—it's far from ideal.' He ran his fingers through his dark hair. 'A little more than three years ago my wife Tabitha and I had IVF via the clinic you'd registered with. My wife didn't have any viable eggs of her own, so we had to opt for a donor. The donor we picked was you.'

His clear blue eyes were fixed on hers. And for some reason they were distracting her. They were darker than she'd first thought. Like deep, tropical pools. A girl could get lost inside a set of eyes like that.

What's more, he was deadly serious. This guy wasn't some nut job. Some crazy stalker from a website. Dan would never have let her leave with anyone like that. Dan trusted this guy. He trusted him to look after her. But Dan had no idea about the other stuff, the underlying current between them.

Lily bit her lip. This was it. This was where she found out if something had gone wrong with one of her eggs— one of this couple's embryos.

Carter stared at his hands. 'IVF didn't work out. It was a strain on our marriage, and we split up shortly afterwards.'

Lily was shocked. This wasn't what she'd expected to hear. 'I'm sorry,' she mumbled. 'I thought you wanted to talk to me about a baby.'

'I do.' His words were abrupt.

'I don't understand...'

Carter pulled an envelope from his pocket. He handed the letter to Lily. It was rumpled—as if it had been pulled from his pocket on numerous occasions—and dated two weeks ago. But why were her hands trembling?

She took the letter and with the first few words let out a gasp, her eyes skimming the page.

Dear Mr Carter

It is with much regret we write to you...never happened before in our establishment...one of your embryos has been implanted into another client... this was only discovered when we went to destroy your embryos as previously agreed...unfortunately this coincided with our other client having a detailed scan of their baby...I would advise at this time you deal with our legal counsel...

Her head felt as if was swimming, treading water and trying frantically to keep above the surface. The words stuck in her throat. What could she even say? She couldn't even begin to understand how he felt.

'But how on earth did this happen? They have failsafes for this.'

'Human error.' The words were practically spat out.

'Poor woman...' Lily's voice trailed off.

'What?' Carter's voice echoed around the truck.

Lily shook her head. 'Do you know how hard it is to get pregnant with IVF? What's her circumstances? She's just found out she's carrying someone else's baby. A baby she probably has no legal rights to. How must she feel? How does her husband feel? Have you considered her at all?'

Carter shook his head. 'I can't believe your first thoughts are for her.' He gritted his teeth. 'This is my baby. My baby that has been wrongly implanted into someone else. My baby, my sperm.'

Lily shook her head. 'It's so much more than that.' She waved the letter at him. 'What does this mean? It says here your embryos were supposed to be "destroyed",' she raised her fingers in the air and made quotation mark signs.

Carter sighed. This was harder than he'd thought. He'd imagined meeting Lily and persuading her to stand next to him in court, with the hope of gaining custody of his baby. The last thing he'd expected was for her to go to bat for the opposition.

How could he expect her to understand? She looked as if children were the last thing on her mind. What kind of a woman drove a Ducati and spent her life doing parachute jumps? Was she really the best person to be standing in a courtroom next to him? Maybe his attorney had got it wrong. Maybe he would be better off on his own.

What on earth had made her donate her eggs? The thought pricked his mind. Maybe if he could get to the bottom of that, he would understand her a little better, and understand how she could help his case.

'I didn't have a choice about destroying the embryos. We'd had them fertilised purely for the purpose of using them in our marriage. My marriage was over—it wasn't appropriate to use them now. That—and the fact I've no idea where Tabitha is.'

The penny dropped in Lily's mind. 'So I'm your backup plan?' She looked indignant.

Carter sighed and started the pick-up again, pulling onto the smooth freeway towards the hospital. Lily was going to be difficult. How on earth was he going to persuade her to help?

'What made you be an egg donor?' Maybe if he could distract her, turn the attention onto herself, it could work in his favour. Maybe if she remembered why she'd donated eggs in the first place, she might be more sympathetic to his plight.

Lily jerked in her seat, as if the question had caught her unawares. Her head went downwards, facing her lap. 'It seemed like a good idea at the time. I had some student debts to pay. Ivy League colleges aren't cheap.'

Carter resisted the urge to slam on the brakes. 'You donated your eggs for money?' This was even worse than he'd thought possible. A woman who donated eggs for money would never evoke the sympathy of the court.

'Yes…and no. It's private.' Lily turned her head and looked out of the window at the passing traffic, clearly signalling the conversation was over.

But Carter was having none of it. 'Well, since we selected you as our egg donor, I guess I feel I'm entitled to know. I need your help Lily. Right now, you're probably the only person who can help me get my child back. I can't find my ex-wife, so you're the next best thing. I'm well aware you might not be interested in children, but I'd hoped, as an egg donor, you might be able to say something in my favour. Anything. That you donated your eggs to give childless couples like us a chance. That you believe in families as much as I do. That you know we were screened by the clinic and went through all the psychological profiling to ensure we were ready. Anything—but you did it for the money'

'Don't make it sound like that,' she snapped.

'Sound like what? You sold part of your body for profit?'

'How dare you?'

'Oh, I dare! I dare, because right now I see my chance to be a father floating out the window because some money-grabber won't help me. I see my flesh and blood being brought up by complete strangers because of a human error.' He thumped his hand on the steering-wheel. 'This is my child. Mine. I want nothing more than to be a good father. Is that too much to ask in this life?'

Lily shrank back into her seat. This wasn't going well

at all. How could she explain to him why she'd done it? Who did this man think he was to ask her questions and stand in moral judgement over her? He had no right!

'Listen, Mr Perfect. You track me down at an airfield and spring this on me. You distract me when I'm due to land and make me injure myself. You know nothing about me. Nothing. And I'm quite sure that there was a clause in the clinic's agreement that said you couldn't track me down—no matter what the reason. So, how dare you?' Her voice rose in pitch. 'How dare you think you have a right to stand in judgement over me? You've no idea what my reasons were for donating eggs and I'm sure as hell not going to tell you!' She folded her arms firmly across her chest. 'Now drop me off at the ER and leave me alone.'

'Not a chance.' The words came out like bullets from a gun.

Deep frown lines etched Lily's head. She lifted her fingers and massaged the sides of her temples, taking a few deep breaths. 'Do you know what, John Carter? I don't need this right now. I don't need the stress of this. I'm sorry. I'm sorry this has happened to you. But to be frank...' she took a deep breath, because right now she'd nothing to lose '...if this is the way you spoke to your wife, I'm not surprised she's currently MIA.'

Carter's brow wrinkled. 'MIA?'

'Missing in action.' Lily sighed.

A smile danced across Carter's lips. He couldn't help it. Her bolshiness amused him. She didn't seem to care that right now he could throw open the door of the pick-up and leave her and her busted ankle stranded at the side of the road. She didn't seem to know how to keep her mouth in check. She just said whatever she felt. And he liked that. He liked that a lot.

She stopped gazing at the freeway for a moment and stared at him again. 'What's with the super-dad clause anyway? Most young, handsome guys I know would run a mile from something like this. Most guys your age are out sowing their wild oats rather than trying to create their own personal football team. What gives?'

Carter's head turned like a shot. 'You think I'm handsome?'

'Did I say that?'

'Yes, you did.' The smirk stretched over his face.

'It's the headache.' She pressed her fingers to her temples again, then looked down towards the floor. 'That, and the supposed broken ankle that I have.' She glanced at the passing road signs. 'How much longer till we get there?'

'You didn't answer the question. Do you think I'm handsome?' He wasn't letting her off that easily.

'Let it go, John.' She emphasized the word heavily, relying on the fact he'd remember they weren't friends.

'Why should I? It's not every day I get called handsome.' He signalled and shifted into the other lane of the freeway, getting ready to take the next exit road. 'And I'm not trying to be super-dad. I've done the wild oats things, it bored me. The one thing I've always wanted was to have a family.' He shrugged his shoulders. 'What's wrong with that?' He shot her a cheeky glance. 'Women don't always get to have the monopoly on wanting a family and having a biological clock that ticks. I want to be young enough, and healthy enough, to play with my kids—not watch from the rocker on the porch.'

Lily gave an involuntary snigger. The image in her mind of an elderly and grey-haired John Carter sitting on his rocker on the porch was too much for her.

He pulled up outside the ER and reached into his

pocket. 'Now, whether you like it or not, I hate to break it to you...' he glanced at his watch '...but as of approximately ten minutes ago I'm the orthopaedic surgeon on call today.' He waved his pager at her. 'So unless you want to go to the other side of the city, you're going to have to let me treat you.'

Lily bit her lip. 'I'm trying to shake you off, not form a permanent attachment to you.'

Carter swung his legs out of the truck and walked round, opening her door. 'Oh, I think you're already too late for that, missy.'

He pulled over a nearby wheelchair and helped her into it. 'Do you want me to find you another doctor, Lily?'

She pretended to pause for a second, as if contemplating the idea, then shook her head. 'There might be benefits to knowing the boss.' She smiled. 'You know, better menus, faster treatment.' She lifted her hands again. 'Something for a headache.'

Carter nodded and wheeled her inside, positioning her chair at the reception desk so she could give her details. He walked inside to the locker rooms and pulled on a set of scrubs and his coat, washing his hands at a nearby sink and squirting them with antibacterial scrub. By the time he came back out, his pager was sounding and Lily was being wheeled into a nearby cubicle by one of the nursing staff.

The nurse looked over, 'Wow! That was fast. I just paged you.'

Carter smiled. 'I've started picking up patients in the street and bringing them in with me.' He nodded at Lily, before picking up her paperwork. 'I've already examined Ms Grayson's ankle, so I'm just going to send her through for an X-ray.'

'It's Saturday afternoon—there's bound to be a queue,' shot back the nurse.

'That's why I'm taking her myself,' said Carter, as he caught the handles of her wheelchair and pushed her off in the opposite direction. 'We'll be back in ten minutes, Jan.'

The nurse shrugged her shoulders and wrote Lily's name up on the nearby whiteboard. It was one less thing for her to do.

Ten minutes later Lily's headache was getting worse. Carter had placed the film on the light box and the fracture was clear, even to a theatre nurse like her.

She groaned. 'I was sure it was just sprained. This is a nightmare.'

Carter shot her a sympathetic look. 'When was the last time you ate?'

'What?'

'Did you have lunch today at the airfield?'

Lily shook her head. 'Last thing I had was breakfast this morning—around seven a.m. Why?'

'Because I need to take you to Theatre.' He pointed at the screen. 'I'm hoping the bone will manipulate back into place, but if it doesn't we might need to pin and plate it.'

Lily felt her stomach drop. She'd worked in Theatre long enough to know what was coming next. 'And if you can manipulate it?'

'Whether we manipulate back into place or pin and plate it, you'll need a cast for around six weeks. First few weeks will have to be non-weight-bearing. If everything goes well, after that we might be able to give you a weight-bearing cast in three or four weeks.'

Lily groaned. 'I can't be off work for six weeks.'

'Where do you work?'

Lily rolled her eyes. 'Theatre, in the Western.'

Carter felt himself come to a complete halt. He had some really good friends who worked there. And who could probably give him a whole host of background information on Lily. 'Have you always worked there?' he queried. His mind was working overtime. When he'd tried to track down Lily, he'd known she was registered as a nurse but hadn't realised she was so close. It could have saved him some precious time and expense.

Lily shook her head. 'I've only worked there for the last six months. And you can imagine—as a theatre nurse, the last place on earth I want to be is inside a theatre.'

Carter shrugged, although he appreciated the sentiment. Hospitals weren't his favourite places either. Working there was fine, but as a patient or a visitor? No, thanks.

'It could be worse—you could be going to your own theatre. The place where you know which surgeons you'd never let operate on you, and which nurses you'd want nowhere near you in Recovery. At least here you don't have any preconceived ideas.'

Lily grimaced. 'I also don't have any faith in the people who'll be looking after me.' She pointed upwards. 'Let me see that X-ray for myself.'

Carter smiled. 'What? You don't trust me? You think I've just pencilled in a little fracture just for the sheer hell of it?' He pulled the film from the light box and handed it down to her.

Lily frowned and held it up towards the nearby window. The fracture was definitely there. No matter which way she turned the X-ray. She sighed and handed the film back to Carter.

'I'm not sure about you being my doctor.'

Carter looked at her steadily. 'What, exactly, do you mean by that?' Was she questioning his competence or his intentions? Either way, he didn't intend to let her off with it.

There was a glint in her eye. 'If you fix my ankle, then that's all you do—fix my ankle. I don't want to be held hostage here until I give in to your other demands—whatever they may be.'

Carter felt himself ready to explode, then he caught the smile stealing across her face. She was toying with him.

He sat down in the chair next to her and shot her a look of pure sincerity, 'Are you questioning my integrity, Nurse Grayson? I am the only orthopod on call this weekend. I could happily leave your ankle until another doctor is on duty on Monday.' His tone was teasing. A plan was beginning to formulate in his mind. Having Lily off her feet for six weeks might actually suit him, and his case, perfectly.

The last thing he wanted a judge to hear was that his egg donor was a crazy, fly-by-the-seat-of-her-pants action junkie. Parachuting wasn't her only unusual activity. The list the PI had given him had sent a shiver down his spine—free-climbing, bungee-jumping, waterskiing and cliff-diving—not least because he knew that at some point he'd tried most of those himself.

Under normal circumstances he might have relished the fact of meeting an adrenaline junkie like himself. But these weren't normal circumstances. And an adrenaline junkie was the last thing he needed.

What he needed was a traditionalist.

And what he'd got was Lily Grayson. A headache waiting to happen.

Maybe he could keep her in a cast for even longer than

six weeks. Long enough for her court appearances at his side, helping him build a case for his baby.

Lily gave him an impatient smile. 'I don't know what's going on inside that head of yours, John Carter, but I don't think I'm going to like it.' She crossed her arms across her chest. 'Not one bit.'

Carter stuck out his hand towards her. 'At some point, Lily, we need to talk. But for now you're my patient. Deal?'

She looked suspiciously at the extended hand in front of her. Large hands. Short, clean fingernails and an extremely steady hold.

She gave a quirky smile and stuck her tiny hand in his. 'Deal, but thank goodness you're not a gynaecologist.'

He looked bewildered. 'What do you mean by that?'

She laughed. 'If I have to explain that to you, cowboy, there's something definitely wrong with this arrangement!'

He shook his head as the taunt finally registered in his brain. 'I'm off to arrange Theatre for you.' He looked at the clock. 'Shouldn't be more than an hour.' He wagged a finger at her. 'Don't go anywhere.'

She raised her hands in exasperation. 'As if I could!' Then leaned back against the pillows. 'And make it quick, John, because I'm starving!'

The words echoed in his ears as he strode down the corridor. Lily Grayson was going to be a challenge.

CHAPTER THREE

CARTER sat in the dimly lit room, slouched in one of the easy chairs, with his feet stretched out and resting on the bed in front of him.

Lily had proved troublesome. It was already getting to be a habit. But at least it had given him a chance to think.

How was he going to persuade the Dynamo to help him? The purple flight suit with neon pink writing was folded on the chair next to him. It represented her perfectly.

His attorney had been clear. Find her and persuade her to appear in court. Even though he was the genetic parent of this child, it wasn't an automatic conclusion he would be awarded custody.

The whole situation was overwhelming.

If the truth be told, he'd always imagined the fairy-tale. The husband, the wife, the nice house and the kids. He'd thought Tabitha wanted that too. That's why they'd created the embryos. And giving the clinic permission to destroy them had felt like the final nail in the coffin. His final failure. No wife. No kids. And no clue what to do next.

This whole thing confused him. At first he'd felt anger—been consumed with rage that such a mistake could be made. Then he'd been overcome with the emotions that this was his child. His flesh and blood.

But Lily's words had surprised him. Her immediate thoughts had been for Olivia, the woman carrying his child. And they'd triggered a whole host of little voices in his head.

He'd been here all night because his patient had needed him. What would he do when he was a single parent with a baby at home? How would he cope with the long hours at work? He'd never considered anything like that. He'd always expected kids to be part of a partnership. He'd never really imagined that he would be doing this himself. Was he good enough? Was he ready?

Carter gave himself a shake. Other single parents managed. He had plenty of colleagues who managed to juggle their work commitments and childcare. He would manage too.

He looked at the sleeping figure on the bed, her chest rising and falling gently, her skin clear and unlined. To all intents and purposes, it was almost as if she didn't have a care in the world.

Now he just had to persuade Lily to help him.

Lily woke up feeling groggy. Her eyes flickered open and her stomach grumbled loudly. She was utterly starving.

Something shifted at the side in her peripheral vision. A green set of scrubs, white coat and dark hair, coupled with a pair of long legs that were stretched out and resting at the bottom of her bed.

On a normal day, this might have been part of a pleasant daydream. But this wasn't a normal day. She knew exactly why John Carter was here—and it was nothing to do with the underlying current between them.

'What is this?' she mumbled. 'The local pit stop?'

Carter jerked to attention, pulling his legs down from the bed. The newspaper that was resting on his lap slid to the floor as he adjusted his rumpled clothing.

'You're awake. At last.' He glanced at his watch.

'What's that supposed to mean?'

He frowned at her. 'When was the last time you had a general anaesthetic?'

She wrinkled her brow. 'I'm not sure. I don't know if I've ever had one.'

Carter leaned forward and touched her arm. 'Well, just for future notice, Ms Grayson, you don't react well to general anaesthetics. You managed to give us quite a scare.'

'I did?' Lily was confused. Something about this whole day didn't seem quite right. The last thing she remembered she was being wheeled into Theatre and it was around four p.m. So why was the sun streaming through the windows like that?

'What time is it?' she asked, trying to make sense of her surroundings.

Carter didn't need to look at his watch again. 'It's just before seven.'

'In the evening?' Surely the sun wasn't that bright in the early evening?

He shook his head. 'Nope. You've slept right through the night. No wonder your stomach is growling. Want me to get you something to eat?'

'I slept right through?' Lily shook her head. She couldn't believe it. She worked in Theatre every day. Her procedure was a straightforward one. She should have been in and out in an hour.

She pushed herself up in the bed, feeling the restriction of the lightweight cast on her leg. 'What on earth happened?'

Carter gave her a smile. He looked shattered. He must have stayed with her all night. He was still wearing yesterday's scrubs and there was a faint hint of stubble around his chin.

'You happened.' He shook his head. 'I don't know why I'm surprised. You don't seem to do anything like you should.'

Lily stared down at the lump under the covers. 'Break it to me gently—am I going to spend the rest of my life setting off airport security alarms with my pin and plate?'

Carter smiled and shook his head. 'A common misconception. Anyway, you didn't need them, the bone manipulated back into place easily.' The glint appeared in his eye again. 'At least one part of you is co-operative.'

Lily rolled her eyes. 'Ha-ha.' Her stomach grumbled loudly again. 'Make yourself useful,' she grumbled, 'and get me some tea and toast.' She looked up at the bag of IV fluids hanging above her and irritating the vein in her wrist. 'I want to get these down as soon as possible.'

He nodded and picked the newspaper off the floor, placing it on his chair as he walked over to the doorway and spoke to one of the nursing aides.

The headline was screaming at her: EMBRYO MIX-UP, DISASTER AT SAN FRANCISCO CLINIC.

She felt her stomach turn over as small pieces of yesterday started to fall into place.

She picked up the paper. 'Lily…' he started.

'Shh.' She put her finger to her lips and started to read.

The words were every bit as bad as she feared.

Disaster has struck at a local and usually highly regarded fertility clinic in San Francisco. Olivia

Simpson and her husband had stored embryos
after his diagnosis with cancer. Mr Simpson died
three years ago and his wife recently underwent
embryo implantation to fulfil their dreams of a
family. Imagine her horror when a detailed scan
revealed the child she was carrying could not possibly be her husband's. Dr John Carter and his wife
Tabitha had stored embryos using an egg donor.
These embryos were due to be destroyed after the
breakdown of their marriage. Instead Dr Carter
was notified via the clinic's attorney that another
woman was now carrying his child.

A spokesperson from the clinic said, 'We are
devastated by these events. We have procedures
and protocols in place to ensure careful han-
dling of all embryos. Never, in the history of our
clinic, have we ever had any incidents like this.
Our thoughts are, at present, with the individuals
affected by this event. Our attorneys are dealing
with our clients in the most sensitive way they can.
Olivia Simpson is distraught. She had expected this
baby to be a lasting legacy to her husband, and Dr
Carter has already expressed his intention to gain
custody of his child.'

'Wow.' Lily sat the newspaper down. 'Looks like I've
missed the most important event.'

Carter bit his lip and sagged back down into the chair
beside her. 'Piranhas,' he muttered at the newspaper.

'They make you sound like a complete and utter—'

'What?' He sat bolt upright in his chair, cutting off
her final word. 'What do you mean?'

Lily pointed at the paper again. 'This makes you
sound unsympathetic—callous even. This poor woman

has lost her husband and thought she was carrying his child. Turns out the child is someone else's. A child she has no biological connection to. Why would she want to continue with this pregnancy? Why would she want to be used as a human incubator and not get anything at the end of it?'

Carter could feel a red, prickling rash creeping up his neck. He hated this. He didn't want to see it from someone else's point of view. He hated Lily feeling empathy towards this woman. This was his child.

'Wait a minute.' Lily fixed him with her steely glare, panic in her voice. 'What's wrong, Carter? What's wrong with your baby that they found out at the scan?'

Every hair on his body stood instantly on end. Orthopaedics was his field, not obstetrics. Apart from the IVF, he could write what he knew about obstetrics on the back of a postage stamp. Although he'd had to learn the basics for his medical qualification, it just hadn't been his forte. He had the sudden feeling he should have paid more attention.

'What are you saying?'

'What has your attorney told you?'

'Very little. I knew the name of the woman—Olivia Simpson. I know she's thirty-six, a widow and an ER resident. Pretty much what you see in the paper. Why? What should I be asking?'

'How far into the pregnancy is she?'

'Thirty weeks. They discovered it at a twenty-eight-week scan. I found out just over a week ago.'

'Don't you get it, Carter? That's just it. What did they discover?'

A deep sinking feeling filled his stomach.

'They didn't just run a transducer across her stomach and say, "This baby looks like John Carter." There has to be a clinical or medical reason for this discovery. That's what you need to know.' The frustration on Lily's face was evident. 'What has your attorney been doing?'

'Advising me on how to make the best case for gaining custody of this baby. First, we tried to track down Tabitha, and when that didn't work, we tried to find you.'

'Call me old-fashioned, John, but what your attorney should have been doing is finding out how your baby is. He should be finding out more about this woman. Is there a chance she'll take action now she knows the baby isn't hers?'

Carter paled visibly. 'What do you mean? She's passed the point where she can do anything. She's too far on to have a termination.'

Lily shook her head. 'What about her state of mind? She might not be able to have a termination, but this baby isn't hers. She doesn't have a vested interest in this child.' Lily flung her arms outwards. 'She could go and drink a bottle of whisky a day. Smoke sixty cigarettes a day. Throw herself down a flight of stairs. Go and jump out of a plane.'

Their eyes met. Silence filled the room as the enormity of the words sank in. Carter looked as if he was going to be sick. Beads of sweat broke out on his brow.

'I'm sorry, John, but I think you need a reality check. Just because this baby is the most important thing in the world to you, it doesn't mean she feels the same.' Lily shifted uncomfortably on the bed. 'What happened to her own embryos? Does she still have a chance of having her husband's baby?'

'I don't know. I've no idea. I never thought to ask any of those questions.' He ran his fingers through his thick, dark hair, then rested his head in his hands. His brain was flooded with a whole maelstrom of jumbled thoughts. The tiny queries and doubts he'd had a few moments ago were all instantly pushed to the side at the thought of someone harming his baby.

'John, you came to me for help. But the help you want is someone to stand next to you in a courtroom and look pretty. As a fellow professional, I have to be honest, the help you need is some better advice.' Her brow wrinkled. 'Why haven't you done the most obvious thing in the world—why haven't you spoken to Olivia Simpson?'

He sighed and ran his fingers through his thick hair. 'If only it was that easy.'

'But it is that easy, John. Pick up the phone and see how she feels. Ask her if she'd be willing to give you custody of the child. You might be working yourself into a frenzy about nothing.'

He shook his head. 'My attorney is dealing with everything. And the one thing he categorically forbade me to do was contact Olivia Simpson. He said it could be seen as harassment and wouldn't help my court case at all. I've got to leave her alone. I can't approach her at all.'

The door opened and one of the nursing aides bustled in, carrying a plate heaped with buttered toast and a mug of tea. 'Here you go,' she said brightly, putting the plate and mug on the bed table and pushing it up towards Lily. Her head flicked from side to side at the obvious tension in the room. She took a step towards the door and then hesitated. 'Lily, is everything okay?'

Lily nodded silently, her eyes still fixed on Carter. He looked in shock. It was as if tiny pieces of the puzzle were slotting into place for him.

The nursing aide lifted the buzzer from the wall and placed it in Lily's hand, her eyes glancing back over to Carter. 'Call me if you need anything,' she said reassuringly, before she left the room with one final glance over her shoulder.

Lily sagged back against her pillows. Her stomach grumbled loudly. She was absolutely starving and the aroma of hot buttered toast was assaulting her senses. But right now it didn't seem appropriate to start eating, with Carter sitting there with a face so pale he could have blended into the surrounding white walls.

'John,' she whispered.

Her voice seemed to startle him. He stood up and started pacing around the room. 'I need to speak to my attorney again,' he mumbled, as if he was talking to himself. He walked in circles, scribbling things down on a piece of paper he pulled from his pocket.

'John.' This time her voice was sharp, determined. Her eyes were steely again. 'Sit down.' She pointed back at the chair and waited until he was sitting until she lifted a piece of toast to her mouth, chewing and swallowing quickly.

'Before you do another thing you can sign my discharge papers. I want to get out of here today and you...' she nodded at him '...are my doctor. So hurry up and pass me fit to leave.'

He shook his head. His brain might be scrambled right now with wrongly implanted embryos and the roles and responsibilities of his attorney, but this kind of thing was second nature to him. 'You had a reaction to your anaesthetic—you need to be monitored for another few hours.' He pointed at her IV fluids. 'You can't be discharged until your IV fluids are down, you're eating and drinking properly, I know that you've passed urine, you're safe to mobilise on crutches and I know you've got adequate support at home.' He'd counted the reasons off on his fingers, then folded his arms across his chest and looked at her again. 'Until I'm happy with all of these things, you're going nowhere.'

Lily could feel the frustration build in her chest. She lifted the mug of tea and took a quick gulp. 'You've seen me eat and drink, so you can take the IV fluids down now. And if you give that nursing aide a shout for me, I'll go and pass urine right now.' She nodded towards the *en suite* bathroom.

She was trying to be smart. She was hoping that he'd be so caught up in his worries about the baby he'd forget about her. The last thing she wanted to do was stay in hospital. Hospitals were fine for working in, but Lily hated the idea of being a patient. And she didn't want him to ask too many questions about help at home. The image of her trying to get up three flights of stairs on crutches was making her feel feel nauseous. The less he knew, the better.

'Give me a minute,' he said, pushing open the door and heading outside.

Lily pulled back the covers and swung her legs to the side of the bed. The room started spinning and she felt herself sway from side to side. She leaned on the bed table for support, taking a deep breath and waiting for the room to settle back into place. After a few seconds the spinning stopped and she bent forward to examine her cast. It was the usual lightweight fibreglass one, from her toes to just under her knee. A smile crept across her face. Someone had decided to give her a bright purple cast—one that matched the colour of her flight suit perfectly. Now, who could that someone have been?

She sighed, and then picked up the newspaper again. Something was making her stomach churn, and she could have put money on it that it wasn't the effects of the anaesthetic.

This was an out-and-out disaster. If she'd met John Carter in normal circumstances she would have been quite taken with him. Tall, dark, handsome and single— what more did a girl need?

Then there was the added extra of him being a fellow adrenaline junkie. In lots of ways John Carter could be the perfect man for her. But then there was his outright confession that he wanted to have a family. Not entirely normal for a man his age. Particularly a heterosexual man his age in San Francisco. They were a fairly rare breed, and adding in the fact he wanted children, she was surprised she couldn't see the long line of potential brides snaking their way down the hospital path.

She had to be missing something.

Her fingers touched the newsprint again. She'd heard of things like this happening before. She'd seen the news reports and read the magazines left in hospital waiting rooms. But none of those stories had affected her. None of those stories had been about her eggs.

Anger rose in her chest. Why hadn't the clinic let her know? They must have known she would read about it in the press. They must have known John Carter might try and track her down. Her grandmother had always told her that forewarned was forearmed and she couldn't have felt less prepared if she'd tried.

Almost as soon as she had the thoughts, she could hear the smooth voice of the clinic's general manager in her ear. 'You signed away your rights when you do-nated the eggs, Ms Grayson'. But these were exceptional circumstances. Nobody could have predicted this would happen. Not even in a bad Sunday afternoon movie.

The egg donation was supposed to have been simple. Go through the screening, get accepted. Put yourself through the procedures a few times and leave a lasting legacy for some couples who wanted a family.

And get to pay off some of your debts.

She cringed. She could almost hear John Carter's voice in her ear again. The shock that someone would donate eggs for money.

Not everyone had the benefit of the privileged upbringing that he had. Not everyone could automatically afford an Ivy League education. But when you'd set your heart on it from an early age, and could easily make the academic grades…

There were plenty of world-renowned nursing colleges across the US. But there was only one Ivy League college that did nursing and that's where Lily had been determined to go. No matter what the cost.

And she wasn't the only one. Seven other girls in her class had gone down the egg donation route. All had had different reasons. And Lily wouldn't have dared ask what they were—not when she played her own cards so close to her chest.

Stephanie, her sister, was fifteen years older and had suffered an early menopause. The effect on her mental health had been devastating. And Lily hadn't been in a position to help.

There was no clinical reason to believe she would have an early menopause. Indeed, all the tests the clinic had carried out on her had been extremely positive. But egg donation was a lasting legacy. She could help others and leave herself a security blanket in the meantime.

Something else struck her. If the clinic had mixed up the Carter's embryos with someone else's, did that also mean they might have misplaced her other eggs? Her security blanket? The thought chilled her to the bone. She needed to get access to a phone.

The door opened and John Carter came back in. He didn't look happy.

'I can't get hold of my attorney and I think you're trying to pull the wool over my eyes, Ms Grayson.'

Lily's heart thudded in her chest. Had he found out about her own egg storage? Surely that was none of his business?

'What do you mean, Dr Carter?'

Carter looked at her legs, one clad in bright purple, dangling over the side of the bed. 'It seems you're pretty well known about these parts.'

Lily shifted uncomfortably. 'What does that mean?'

Carter looked stern. 'It means that I've found out your apartment is three flights up and you live alone. I've also checked and there are no elevators and no concierge. So tell me, Miss Grayson…' he moved over closer to her, lowering his head to face hers '…how exactly were you going to manage when you got discharged later today?'

Relief flooded through her. This she could deal with. This would be a breeze. She waved her arms in the air, 'Once the physio passes me as fit on the crutches, I'll get the cab driver to help me up the flights of stairs to the apartment—easy!'

Carter's brow wrinkled. 'Do you live in the same city of San Francisco that I do? How many cab drivers do you know that'll leave their cab to help someone up three flights of stairs?'

Lily shrugged. 'I'll pay him extra.'

'And what happens when you get there? When you get up those flights of stairs and are left in the apartment?' He pulled his chair over until he was sitting completely in front of her. 'You do realise that once you start using these crutches, that's it? You won't even be able to make yourself a coffee and carry it through your apartment—you'll be stuck in your kitchen, balancing while you drink it.' He eyed her carefully. 'You'll need help getting in and out of the shower, and you won't be able to carry a plate through your house. Where are you going to eat? How are you going to manage your shopping?' He tapped the crutches he'd carried in with him. 'All your weight will be resting on these, and you won't have a free hand to do anything.'

Something happened. Something changed. It was as if a little light had gone on inside Carter's head. A smug expression came across his face. He folded his arms across his chest and rested the crutches at the side of the bed. 'You need help, Lily Grayson.'

Lily felt something sweep across her skin like a cool breeze. A strange discomfort. She had the impression this wasn't going to end well.

She was also having visions of her broken shower that she'd spent the last month meaning to get fixed. She might be able to wrap her leg in a plastic garbage bag and tape it closed for a few minutes to step in the shower, but she certainly couldn't jump in and out of the bath the way she'd done for the last month.

She barely knew any of the neighbours in her apartment block. There were a few residents she recognised and would say hello to on the stairs. But there certainly wasn't anyone she could ask to help her in the bathroom.

Carter was still staring at her with that smug grin on his face. 'So what if I need help?' she snapped. Lily hated things being out of her control. She hated the thought of needing help.

'This is simple,' said Carter. 'I need help, you need help.' He shrugged his shoulders. 'Why don't we just help each other?'

The words hung in the air.

Lily felt as if she couldn't breathe. He was close to her again, so close she could smell his ocean aftershave and see the individual stubble hairs around his chin. The whole essence of him seemed to sweep around her, sending lightning sensations down her spine. Was this still the effects of the anaesthetic? Or was this just him?

Although the sun was streaming through the windows, Lily felt as if she was in a darkened nightclub, with a low, thumping beat in the background. The last time she'd felt like this, she'd been in a bar, her senses interrupted by two glasses of wine and the large shape of a gorgeous man in front of her.

But that had been months ago, and the man had vanished as quickly as he'd appeared.

This was different. This was the cold, hard light of day.

This was a man who had expectations of her. Expectations that she wasn't sure she wanted to fulfil. Her judgement felt clouded. She couldn't think straight when she was around him. And she certainly didn't want to feel indebted to him.

'What exactly do you mean, John?'

His brow furrowed. 'And will you quit the "John". I told you, my friends call me Carter.' He stood up again and moved again. 'Lily, if you want me to sign discharge papers for you, I have to know you either have some help—or somewhere more accessible to stay. Do you have a friend you can stay with? Or someone who can come around and give you a hand?'

Lily bit her lip. Her plan hadn't worked. Although she had friends, most of them were nurses and worked a variety of shifts, and most of them lived in apartments similar to hers. None of them lived on the ground floor.

She shook her head, quickly, almost imperceptibly, hoping he wouldn't even notice.

Carter hesitated, just for a second. This could work out well for him, but he was reluctant to take advantage of her. For some reason, no matter how much this could help him, he wanted her to feel free to choose.

'Lily, I've already told you why I need your help. I want to get custody of my baby more than anything in the world. And right now you need some help—the practical kind.' He ran his fingers through his tousled hair. 'I live in a bungalow in one of the city suburbs. I've got three spare rooms, two with *en suite* shower rooms and plenty of space. You could stay with me for the next few weeks until you get your walking cast on. That could be around three or four weeks, depending on how your leg heals. What do you think?'

Carter took a deep breath. Please let her say yes. He tried not to let the stress he was currently feeling show on his face. 'If it helps, you can give me the name of your favourite orthopaedist at the Western and I'll make your follow-up appointment with him. Now I've done your emergency treatment, we can keep the two things totally separate—I won't be your doctor.' He paused for a second, giving her a chance to mull over the options in her head. But he was on a roll now and he didn't want to take the chance that she might not consider helping him. 'I guarantee I won't pressure you into helping me. But I will set out my case to you.' He caught her gaze for a second. 'You've already helped me this morning, you asked me questions that I hadn't thought of myself.' He took a few steps towards the door. 'I don't have anyone else to discuss this with.' He glanced at the newspaper. 'And I certainly don't want to speak to anyone who will go to the press.' He tilted his head to the side and let out a sigh. 'You could be my sounding board, Lily. You could help me see both sides of the story.' His eyes drifted over to the window. 'Because I haven't managed to do that so far. And, in the meantime, you'll get to know me a little better and realise I'm not such a bad guy. Maybe you'll get to understand why I want to be a dad so much.'

His eyes met hers again. Her brown contacts had been removed for Theatre, and her green eyes were unsettling him. He tried to smile. 'What do you say? Will you help me?'

She was frozen at the side of the bed. All of a sudden her dangling legs and theatre gown left her feeling really exposed. There was something so wrong about this. A man she hardly knew was offering to help her. Not only that, he was opening himself up to her.

For a big, hunk of a man John Carter sure looked vulnerable right now. How must he be feeling? Someone else had his baby inside her right now, and he absolutely no control over the situation.

Lily racked her brain. She was sure that in previous cases the biological parents had been successful in getting their baby back. But would the same rules apply to John?

His embryos were due to be destroyed—surely that would go against him? His wife had disappeared, and that wouldn't do him any favours either. Who did he really have on his side? Who did he have for support?

Was this really something she wanted to be involved in? How much help could she be?

What happened if the other attorney looked into her background—and came to the same conclusions that John had, that she'd donated eggs purely for the money? Did she really want her life exposed in that way?

All of these thoughts ploughed around in her brain.

The loudest one screaming Walk away. But she couldn't walk away, could she? Not physically, or figuratively.

Every hair on her body stood on end. Something inside her was drawing her to this man. And it didn't matter that she'd donated eggs, or that he'd come to find her.

She'd have felt like this if she'd met him in the street, or in a bar, or in a restaurant. There was just something there. Something between them.

Could she really walk away from him?

She moved closer to the edge of the bed and he was at her side in an instant. His arm swept behind her waist to support her and he handed her the crutches. The heat enveloped her.

She lifted her head to his. His blue eyes were on her, full of worry but full of hope. She could get lost in those eyes.

A smile broke across her face and it felt like the most natural thing in the world between them. She lifted her lips to his ear and whispered, 'Yes. I'll help you John,' before she changed her mind.

CHAPTER FOUR

LILY sat in the front of the pick-up, her crutches wedged beside her. Walking with crutches had proved a little more troublesome than she'd predicted. As for getting up the stairs... She shuddered at the memory of the hospital physiotherapist catching her before she'd fallen down the few steps she'd managed to climb up.

Carter appeared next to her, opening the door and dumping a large rucksack in her lap. 'Did you get everything?' she asked, as he scooted around and jumped into the driver's seat.

He shot her a wicked grin and handed her back her crumpled list. 'Interesting underwear,' was the instant reply.

'What?' She looked in horror as he gunned the pick-up's engine and drew back out into the San Francisco traffic.

She could feel the colour flush into her cheeks. She screwed the list up in her hand. This was a nightmare. She'd tried to keep the list to a minimum—clothes, toiletries, books, underwear...

She tugged at the zip on her rucksack and instantly saw the flash of a bright pink satin thong. 'Carter!' she shouted, aghast.

'At last.' He smiled.

'What?' She was cringing inside. Of all the under-wear, all the sensible black and white panties and bras she had stuffed in her bedside cabinet, he'd managed to find the secret stash of matching silk sets. He must have done a fair bit of rummaging to come up with those.

'You finally called me Carter—just like my friends do.' His bright white smile filled his tanned complex-ion. He had that wicked gleam in his eye again—and no wonder.

She groaned and he shrugged as he indicated and turned left. 'Hey, I only did what I was told to do—get the things on your list. What's wrong?'

'What's wrong is that you went through my under-wear drawer and brought the most inappropriate un-derwear you could find.' She gave a little gasp as she discovered what was underneath the pink thong. 'Where on earth did you find this?' She pulled a leopard print short satin nightdress from her bag. 'I asked you to bring me pyjamas!'

Carter gave a fake shudder down his spine. 'Yeah, and I found them. They were best left hidden in a drawer.'

Lily was horrified and her face was growing even redder by the second. 'What does that mean?'

'That means that some things should never be shared—especially when they look like that!'

Lily sighed and leaned back in her seat, watching the traffic filter past. What on earth was she doing? Had she really thought this through?

The short answer was no. And although John Carter appeared, to all intents and purposes, a stand-up guy, what would he say if she refused to help him?

He signalled and moved lane following the signs to Hillsborough, a wealthy suburb of San Francisco.

The ideal place. If you could afford it. Far enough

from the city centre to be away from the chaos, but close enough to enjoy all the amenities San Francisco had to offer. She'd dreamed of living in a place like this.

Ten minutes later Carter pulled up outside a house and Lily was momentarily distracted by a kid walking along, pushing a bike. 'Hi, Carter,' came a shout and casual wave on the way past.

'Hi, Donovan,' he responded as he jumped out of the pick-up and came round to open her door.

Lily's mouth was hanging open. 'You live here?' she gasped as she looked around her. The huge curved cul-de-sac was filled with large houses with sweeping driveways, all different in design. Carter's house looked as if it belonged on a Spanish island, the house across the street from Colonial times and the house at the bottom of the cul-de-sac from an English Heritage site.

Lily swung her legs around and positioned her crutches, before jumping down from the pick-up. 'What do you call this place—Billionaire's Row?'

Carter pulled his shoulders back, as if irritated by the barb. 'Not at all, none of the houses cost that much.'

She watched as he grabbed her bag and headed up the carefully laid yellow paved path. These houses were expensive. She could never afford to live in a place like this. But these houses also looked lived in. There were kids' toys all over the front yards, she could see climbing frames, swings and slides sticking up in most of the back yards—probably next to the luxury pools.

'Are you coming or not?' Carter was standing next to his open door, make that his double open doors— trust him to have a doorway you could get an elephant through.

Lily limped up the path. These crutches were definitely going to take some getting used to. She paused at the entrance and peered inside.

'What's wrong?' quipped Carter, 'Nobody's going to bite you.'

She tentatively edged her crutches inside. Just looking at the place made her nervous. The red-tiled floor crossed the huge open-plan room and over into the immaculate stainless-steel kitchen, then up to the glass doors leading out to the swimming pool.

'Wow,' was all she could say.

Carter crossed the room and dumped her bag on the leather sofa before moving over to the kitchen and switching on the deluxe coffee machine. Lily shuddered—she was sure she would break it the first time she touched it.

He picked up a remote and zapped on the huge flat-screen TV that hung above the cream fireplace. 'What do you want to watch?' he asked, as he busied himself at the coffee machine. 'And what do you want to drink— latte, espresso, cappuccino?'

Lily had moved into the middle of the room—her whole apartment could fit into his living room—and her legs started to wobble. She sagged down onto the leather sofa, which instantly seemed to swallow her up. 'Oof!'

'Are you okay?' Carter was at her side in an instant.

She gave a weary smile. 'It was that long, long walk up your path, John. It just finished me off.'

Carter frowned, trying to work out if she was teasing or not. 'Do you want me to show you to your room, do you want to lie down?'

'How many miles will I have to walk to get there?'

Now he knew she was joking, so he played her at her own game and swiftly slid his arms under her, lifting her from the sofa.

'What do you think you're doing?' she shrieked.

Carter smiled as he strode down the hall, 'Don't let it be said I'm not a hospitable host.' He stopped outside a wooden doorway and lifted his foot giving the door a sturdy kick. 'Voilà!'

Lily turned sideways, her arms automatically wrapping around his neck to steady her position. Inside was a beautiful dark wooden four-poster bed with white voile curtains and a white linen bedspread. Wide glass doors looked out over the back yard and swimming pool. There was another flat-screen TV, hung on the wall opposite the bed, and another door leading off to a white and yellow *en suite*.

Carter sat her down at the side of the bed. 'Is this to your liking, Ms Grayson?' he asked. She could hear the pride in his voice. And it wasn't about size or splendour. This was his home. And he loved it.

The natural reaction to make a sarcastic comment stuck in her throat. This wasn't the time for jokes or insults. She pushed herself up the bed and looked at her surroundings. 'This is one of the nicest houses I've ever been in,' she admitted quietly.

A smile instantly rose on his cheeks. 'You like it? Good.' He walked over the glass doors. 'The key is in the lock,' he said, 'and there's a wooden patio table and chair outside if you want some fresh air.' He pointed to the wardrobe. 'I'll bring your clothes in for you and put your toiletries in the bathroom.' He cringed a little. 'I have to admit something to you.'

Lily's eyes narrowed suspiciously. 'I knew this was too good to be true—what is it?'

'I borrowed something from the hospital for you.'

Her tone grew serious. 'John, what did you borrow?'

He raised his eyebrows. 'So, it's back to John, is it?'

He ducked inside the *en suite* and came out carrying a white plastic shower chair—the kind that was normally given to elderly adults with mobility problems. 'I wasn't too sure how you'd manage in the wet room. I didn't want you to slide, so I borrowed a chair.' He held up some garbage bags and duct tape. 'I think I've found everything you'll need, but...' He paused and gave her another of his cheeky grins. 'If you need a hand in there, just let me know.'

Her heart was still fluttering at the mere thought of the wet room. She couldn't wait for him to leave so she could explore it. Lily picked up one of the white stuffed cushions from the bed and flung it at him. He laughed and ducked easily out of its path.

The smile left his face and he walked over to the bed. 'You look tired, Lily. And the reaction you had to the anaesthetic can't be helping. How about I leave you alone and let you sleep?'

The comfortable bed was already calling to her and although it went against all her principles, she took a deep breath and nodded. 'I am quite tired.'

This time the humour was gone from his voice, 'Do you need a hand?'

She shook her head. 'A glass of water and some painkillers would be great, thanks.'

He appeared two minutes later and placed the water and tablets on the bedside cabinet, leaning the crutches against the bed. He opened her bag and handed her the satin nightdress. 'Don't worry—I'll leave before you put it on.' There was a smile on his face and his gaze lingered just a little longer than necessary. Lily could feel their simultaneous unspoken thoughts, both of them wondering what the other would do if he stayed.

Lily reached out and touched his arm. 'What's that?'

she queried, pointing to the pale grey garment holder across his arm.

He straightened the bag and hung it up in the cupboard. 'I brought you a dress.'

'A dress—why?' She pointed down at her purple cast. 'I can hardly wear a dress with this.'

'I want to take you out to dinner—to talk. I thought you might need something to wear.'

Her brow wrinkled. 'I'm not really feeling up to dinner.'

He shook his head. 'I didn't mean tonight—naturally, I planned on letting you settle in. But I thought maybe tomorrow. It would give us an opportunity to talk about things.' She could see him biting the inside of his cheek. He was feeling uncomfortable. 'You can choose where we go. Where do you like? Fisherman's Wharf? Pier 39?'

'Chinatown.' Her answer was instant, with no hesitation whatsoever.

'Chinatown?' he seemed surprised.

She nodded. 'Happy Sam's.'

He seemed a little thrown by her choice, but he nodded thoughtfully, then gave her a little smile. 'Happy Sam's it is.' He headed towards the door.

'And, John?'

'Yeah?' He turned at the doorway. She could see the deep frown lines in his forehead, something she hadn't noticed before, and the dark circles under his eyes. He was stressed. This whole situation was out of his control, and for the first time she felt some sympathy for him.

He may want her help, but he'd bent over backwards for her today. He'd brought her to his home, collected her clothing and even planned ahead and anticipated her care needs. Maybe it was time to cut him a little slack.

She smiled. 'Are you working tomorrow?'

He nodded.

She gave him an even more dazzling smile. 'So you're leaving me alone all day tomorrow in this fancy house?'

'Should I be worried?' His voice rose, joking with her.

'Only if you're leaving that shiny new laptop I saw in the living room—and only if I find your credit card.' Cut him some slack? Never.

He shook his head and walked out of the room, then ducked back around the gap. He wagged his finger at her, 'The credit card? You can have it. But if you break my coffee machine, you're really in trouble.'

He ducked again, as another white pillow went flying past his head.

Lily fingered the soft elegant purple jersey dress he'd picked from her wardrobe. Yet another thing she'd forgotten she owned—probably because she rarely had occasion to wear it. He'd also picked up a pair of purple jewelled flip-flops. Only one would fit, but it would look fine with the dress and the crutches.

Today had been very long and very boring, and her mind was working overtime. She couldn't stand six weeks of this. She couldn't stand being inactive.

There was only so much reality TV a girl could watch. She'd even turned to the shopping channels, but when her hand had hovered near the phone as the infomercial for the new super deluxe six-week gel nail polish reached its peak, she knew her brain had switched off. She was a theatre nurse—she wasn't allowed to *wear* nail polish. At least not on her fingers.

And nothing was straightforward with a cast. The shower had taken her nearly twice as long as she'd hoped. Taping a garbage bag over her cast had proved awkward. Sitting on the shower chair as the freezing water came on reminded her why, as a nurse, she always ran the water for her patients first.

Theatre nurses didn't have much call to help patients wash and it was amazing how quickly you forgot the simple details. The cold water had been a nasty shock to the system.

Getting dried had proved even trickier, and as for styling her hair...thank goodness it was short.

She glanced over at the white bed. Her matching purple silk underwear set was lying on top of the bedspread, willing her to put them on. It should be simple. It made perfect sense. She was wearing a purple dress and shoes. She had a purple cast. It stood to reason she should wear purple underwear.

But something about it felt odd. Almost as if she were willing John Carter to see it. And that left her feeling distinctly uncomfortable.

He wanted her help—that was all. Somehow her anaesthetic-affected brain was reading too much into all this. His thoughtfulness. His smiles. The touch of his hand. She gave herself a shake and pulled her dressing gown off, slipping on her bra and panties before she had time to think about it any more.

There was a strange feeling in her stomach. Just the tiniest bit of unease. She was undeniably attracted to him. But did he feel the same way?

How far would John Carter go to gain her help? Flirting was one thing. But acting on it? Surely not. A shiver stole down her spine and she shook it off. Nothing was going to happen between them. This was stupid.

John had phoned to say he would pick her up in ten minutes. She didn't have time for all this. The jersey dress dropped easily over her slim hips and she slid her single foot into the purple flip-flop.

A little styling product on her blonde hair, a touch of black mascara, cream blusher and pink lip gloss and she was ready.

Her stomach let out a growl. Finding food in John's elegant kitchen had been harder than she'd thought. The man hadn't heard of junk food—the kind of thing you needed when you were stuck at home all day sick, like cookies or chips. And there was no way she touching that oven, with its millions of knobs, all whispering You're about to cause thousands of dollars' worth of damage.

'Is that your own personal siren?'

Lily nearly jumped a foot in the air at the sound of his voice. She spun around as much as she could without falling over. 'Where did you spring from?' He was leaning in the doorway dressed in a casual pale blue shirt and dark trousers, his gaze fixed directly on hers. 'I never even heard you come in.'

'I'm surprised you could hear anything above the noise coming from your stomach.' He took a few steps closer and his eyes swept up and down her curvy frame. 'You're looking good, are you ready to go?' He glanced at his watch. 'Taxi's waiting.'

Her eyebrows shot up. 'We're getting a cab?'

Carter rolled his eyes. 'We're getting a cab. It's been one of those days and I want to relax and have a beer tonight. So, no driving.'

She picked up her bag and stuck her hands back into her crutches, nodding in approval. He wasn't so uptight that he couldn't relax with a drink, but he wasn't too foolish as to consider driving. 'I'm ready,' she said. 'Let's go.'

'Hold on a second, you forgot something.' He walked over to the nearby dresser and picked up the thin silver pendant she'd left sitting out. 'Let me.'

Before she even had a chance to think, he'd undone

the clasp and lifted the pendant over her head, his fingers brushing the base of her neck as he fumbled to fasten it. 'Give me a second. Man hands here, my fingernails aren't long enough for this.'

Lily couldn't breathe. She could give him just as many seconds as he wanted. His fingers ran across the base of her neck again and she bit her bottom lip. Her body was starting to react in a way she didn't want John Carter to find out about.

'There we go. Perfect.' Instead of standing back, he ran his fingers along the length of the chain and down towards the pendant, watching in the mirror and straightening it, before realising it was almost resting between her breasts. He pulled back his hand like a shot. 'Sorry,' he murmured, colour coming to his cheeks.

'That's fine,' said Lily, relieved to see she wasn't the only one flustered by the close contact. This wasn't one-sided. She wasn't imagining things. He was feeling it too.

She stumbled, unused to the balancing act required with having one leg off the floor, her shoulders falling backwards into his firm chest. His arms swept forward around her waist to catch her—to steady her—with his head bending forward over her shoulder. And they froze.

His lips were only an inch from hers. He blinked his eyes and his eyelashes brushed against her brow. She couldn't breathe. Her eyes went from his dark lips to his blue eyes and back again. Would he kiss her? Would he act on this attraction between them? She could feel his fingers pressing at her waist. He hadn't released her yet. The earlier unease had vanished in a flash. This didn't feel staged. He wasn't pretending. No one could pretend this. This was real.

Carter felt caught in a time warp for a second. He could hear her breathe. He could feel the warm air on his skin. If she tilted her chin just a little, her lips would come into contact with his. This was unreal.

To hell with dinner. He could just pick her up and carry her over to the bed right now. He could remove that soft purple dress and find out what she was wearing underneath. It might be one of those silk underwear sets that he'd brought from her secret stash in her apartment. That really set his mind on fire.

But he didn't. He took a deep breath. Tonight was about his baby. Tonight was his chance to persuade Lily to help him. No matter how much testosterone was currently circulating in his blood, he had to do this in a calm and rational manner. No matter how much he wanted to, throwing Lily on to the bed would be something else entirely.

Her eyes were fixed on his. And it was almost as if she could read the wicked thoughts currently flowing through his brain. He smiled at her, brushing his lips close to her neck and whispering in her ear, 'Let's go get this cab,' as he released his fingers from her waist and held out his arm to her.

It only took them fifteen minutes to reach the restaurant and be seated at one of her favourite tables. The waiter recognised her immediately, making a fuss over her crutches and cast.

She didn't even need to pick up the menu. 'What do you want?' She leaned across the table and pulled the menu from his hands. 'Just tell me what you like and they'll make it for you here.'

'Really?' She nodded.

'Then I'll have Chinese sticky beef.'

She gave a little smile. 'Interesting choice. I would have put you down as a curry man.'

The waiter appeared at their side, 'Hi, George, one Chinese sticky beef with rice and one Singapore noodles.'

'And to drink?'

Lily gave him a wide grin. She gestured across the table, 'I think the gentleman is in need of a beer and I'll have a glass of white wine, please.'

The waiter hurried off and Lily leaned back in her chair. He'd almost kissed her. She knew it. And he knew it.

Whatever this was between them, it was real.

And no matter what other circumstances there might be, this felt good.

What would he have done if she'd reacted in the bedroom? What would he have done if she'd lifted her chin and put her lips on his? How would that have turned out?

There it was again. That heat that infiltrated her body whenever she started to have wicked thoughts about John Carter. The delightful little buzz that shot up her spine and set her nerve endings on fire.

The thrill of a new romance. There was nothing like it.

She fingered the white tablecloth in front of her, trying to stop a wicked smile from drifting across her face.

There was plenty of time for those thoughts later. They were in a public place, her favourite restaurant, and it may be a Wednesday night, but the place was packed. Even though they were relatively early, there was already a queue at the door.

She could tell by the look on his face he'd something else on his mind. Something that was obviously circulating round and round. The tiny lines around his eyes were deepening, as if he was preparing to tell her something.

And while she wished it could be about their deepening attraction, she could sense it wasn't.

Carter was looking around him in approval. 'I like this place. How did you find it?'

Lily grinned. 'Believe it or not, I used to work here.'

'What?'

She laughed. 'Don't look like that. Whenever I came home from college, I always needed to find work in the holidays—not all of us live in Billionaire's Row. Happy Sam's was looking for staff.'

Carter's gaze narrowed, 'Do you still get a staff discount?'

'Not when you're paying.' Her response was rapid. 'And you'd better be a good tipper.'

Two minutes later their drinks appeared. Carter took a long swallow and relaxed back into his chair.

'So,' began Lily, 'are you going to tell me what's up?'

Carter let out a sigh, his eyes fixing on the wall behind her. 'I got hold of my attorney today.'

'And?'

He cleared his throat. 'You were right. There is something wrong with the baby. Apparently as the "genetic parent"...' he raised his fingers in the air '...they're supposed to notify me of any potential medical problems with the baby.'

'What kind of wrong?' Almost instantly the tiny hairs on her arms stood on end. Her hand went automatically across the table, her fingers intertwining with his.

'The baby has a type of haemolytic disease—anti-Kell.'

Her nose wrinkled. 'Okay, you've got me. I know next to nothing about obstetrics. You'll need to fill me in.'

Carter nodded. 'That's the trouble. Me too. I spent

half the day looking it up in my old textbooks and trying to contact a friend of mine who's an obstetrician.'

She gave his hand a squeeze. 'So tell me what you do know.'

'It's an incompatibility between the mother's Rh blood group and the foetus. It happens when an Rh-negative mother becomes pregnant with an Rh-positive child.' He pointed at himself. 'I'm Rh positive so the baby has inherited this from me.'

'Okay, so what does incompatible mean? Tell me simply, what does that mean for the baby?'

Carter sat back and released her hand. 'It means the baby has developed anaemia and some cardiac complications. When they scanned the baby they noticed how oedematous it looked. The condition can be life threatening if it's not identified quickly. They had to give the baby an *in utero* blood transfusion.'

Lily jumped as the steaming plates of food were set down before them. She completely ignored them. 'Is the baby at risk? Is there a risk to the mother?'

'Yes and yes.' Carter picked up the nearby set of chopsticks and started pushing his food around the plate without really looking at it. 'These things are usually picked up earlier—most babies are identified around eighteen weeks and have the transfusion then. With IVF, both parents' blood groups are already known so they can screen early for any problems. But Olivia's husband must have been Rh negative, meaning they didn't anticipate any problems. Things just turned out a little differently.' He sighed and put his chopsticks back on the table. 'Apparently it was touch and go.'

Lily could see the worry on his face. 'But that's not your fault, John. None of this is your fault.'

His blue eyes fixed on hers across the table. 'So why does it feel like it is?'

Lily felt all the air rush away from her ears. It was as if all the background noise in the restaurant had disappeared. And their table had been transported into a middle of a field where it was just the two of them. Alone.

She couldn't breathe. There was a pressure against her chest. Her lungs just couldn't suck the air in. Why did it look like John Carter had just bared part of his soul to her? She wasn't ready for this. She wasn't ready for any of this.

She hadn't even agreed to help him yet, but the thought of a sick baby already made her feel guilty. Even though she hadn't had a chance to assess how she felt about any of this yet, those deep blue eyes were making the possibility of her saying no extremely difficult.

He blinked.

That single act broke the spell.

Her eyes went downwards, fixing on her plate. The Singapore noodles were gorgeous and steam was still rising from them. This was her favourite food in the world, and they usually didn't last too long around her.

She lifted her chopsticks and started to twist, then swallowed nervously, 'So what are you going to do? Is your baby going to have ongoing health problems or have they been sorted out now?'

'The transfusion was completed, but there can be problems—heart failure, jaundice, anaemia. All things that need to be monitored when the baby is delivered. And most babies with this disorder are delivered early.'

He finally lifted a piece of the sticky beef to his mouth and took a bite. He sat back in surprise. 'This is really good.' She instantly understood. He was stalling. He was trying to distract himself from the thoughts that must be currently circulating in his head.

She gave him a nod. 'Told you so.'

He played around with his food again. 'I'm going to do the only thing I can do—keep in touch with my attorney. There's no question that this baby is mine and I'm supposed to be kept informed of any problems. At this point I can't interfere, but I should be kept in the loop.'

Lily could see the expression on his face. This guy was just like her. He was used to being in control, being in charge. This was totally alien to him. And it must be infuriating him, every bit as much as it was her. She'd only been on crutches for twenty-four hours and already she was wanted to throw things off the wall. How on earth would she feel in his shoes, knowing that someone else was carrying her baby?

Then it hit her. Someone else was carrying her baby.

She kept thinking about this child as if it were nothing to do with her when biology told her differently. But this child didn't feel like hers. She didn't feel as if she had any investment in this child.

Donating eggs had seemed relatively easy at the time. The physical procedure hadn't been without its difficulties, but she hadn't truly considered the emotional aspects. Then again, never in a million years had she imagined anything like this happening. At the time she'd brushed it off. She was doing something good—something humanitarian for other people. As a bonus, she'd had the opportunity to freeze some of her own eggs for use at a later date if she needed them. And those eggs felt like hers.

She knew which facility they were stored in, how many there were, their grading quality and even the number of the DEWAR storage tank. Because at some point in the future, she might need to rely on those eggs. They were her investment.

She cleared her throat. 'So what are your chances of gaining custody of the baby?'

His eyes narrowed. 'You mean my baby?' The words hesitated on his lips. 'There's been a number of cases in the U.S. But it seems it can go either way—depending on the people involved and the circumstances.'

'How do you feel about that?'

She could see emotion flitting behind his eyes. 'How do you think I feel? One minute I'm planning to bring a baby home and the next, I'm wondering if I'll even get to catch sight of my son.'

Lily paused for a second, as if gathering her thoughts and choosing her words carefully. "You seem a little overwhelmed by all of this. Have you really thought all this through?"

Those blue eyes were on hers again. Staring at her intently. His voice was quiet and measured. 'It's a lot to take in. I guess I'm just trying to take it one day at a time.' She heard the deep intake of breath. 'Sometimes it's easier just to think about something else—even if it's just for a few minutes.'

Carter was eating now. His head was over his plate, obviously deep in thought. Did he realise how that just sounded? Was he using her as a distraction? She took a long gulp of her wine. Panic was starting to eat into her. What was she doing here? Why had she allowed herself to end up in this position?

This wasn't her. Nothing about this was her.

This was all him. For the first time in years she was allowing herself to be influenced by a man. And it frightened her.

It wasn't just about this wrongly implanted embryo. He'd been on her mind all day today. And it unsettled her.

The way she'd watched the door today, wondering when he might return. The way she'd jumped when the phone had rung.

The curious way she'd looked around his house—it was far too good an opportunity to miss—wondering if she would find out anything else about him.

Maybe it was all just information overload. They'd met at the parachute jump and he'd kind of sprung things on her. She'd injured her ankle and hadn't really had time to think about it. Now already she was feeling indebted to him.

She looked over the table. His broad shoulders filled the pale blue shirt. His short dark hair and blue eyes had most of the women in the restaurant sweeping their gazes over him in envy. Even his hands didn't seem quite so large any more...

Then there was the flirting. And the touching. And the almost kiss. And the way he sometimes looked at her. And the way he smiled at her. And the fact he had the same interests as her.

In another world, in another set of circumstances, everything about him could have been perfect. But life didn't work that way, as Lily had learned to her cost when her sister had been unwell. When she'd taken the precautionary step of preserving some of her eggs. Carter already had one broken marriage behind him and, by the sound of it, the stress of the infertility treatments had killed it stone dead. And look at the complications now. This was every man's worse nightmare. There was no way he would ever set foot in an IVF clinic again. And she couldn't blame him. But maybe that meant he wasn't so perfect?

'Lily?' His voice broke into her thoughts, his barely touched food just pushed around his plate. 'This was a bad idea. I'm sorry. I'm not really good company this evening. Do you mind if we leave?'

She reached over and touched his hand. It was an automatic reaction. She had to touch him. She had to offer him some comfort.

There was something in his voice. The strain. The hurt. Her heart squeezed inside her chest.

But attraction was still there. No matter what else was going on around them. And it was bubbling over, ready to erupt.

She nodded automatically and signalled to George for the bill. She pushed her hands down on the table and stood, balancing while she adjusted her crutches. 'Let's go, Carter.'

His hand slid around her waist, steadying her. She lifted her head as his lips brushed against her ear. 'You okay?'

She nodded. She was too aware of his presence. Too aware of the tingles running down her spine. Too aware of his breath at the back of her neck and the fingers at the side of her waist. He pulled her closer to him, allowing a waiter with a loaded tray to slide past, but all she could feel was the heat emanating from his body. His leg against hers, his hip touching her just above the waist.

'Let's grab a cab,' he said, steering her towards the exit and out onto the pavement.

Night had fallen, pooling the streets in darkness. Across Chinatown there were a myriad of coloured lights from all the restaurants, and although the evening was warm, it was late and the light breeze cooled her skin. There was a taxi stand across the street and Carter kept his hand fixed tightly around her waist as she hopped across the road.

They stopped for a second outside one of the cabs. 'What is this, Carter?' She had to ask. She couldn't bear this a moment longer.

His husky voice was at her ear in an instant. 'I don't know. But let's find out before it drives us both crazy.' He yanked open the nearby cab door.

She climbed inside the dark cab and rested back on the leather seat. Carter pulled the door closed and gave directions to the taxi driver. His hand rested on her leg.

Lily felt herself hold her breath. A thousand snappy comments filled her brain, but none of them seemed appropriate. The only sound was the light hum of music coming from the radio.

She couldn't help herself. Her mouth worked quicker than her mind. 'That's a bit forward for someone I've just met.'

Carter jerked, nearly pulling his hand away at her words. In this dim light her eyes sparkled with every passing streetlight. The glint in them wasn't shocked or horrified, it was taunting him. Trying to see how far he would go.

His fingers tightened on her thigh and he tilted his head. 'We haven't just met. I'd say this was pretty sedate for someone I met four days ago.'

'It's not been four days—it's only been three.' She smiled. 'You really can't add, can you?'

Carter glanced at his watch and shook his head. 'A day at the airfield, a day in hospital and a day at home. Right now, it's officially two minutes after midnight. That makes it day four.'

Lily opened her mouth to argue. If they were taking it from the moment they'd met at the airfield, it wasn't officially four days yet. But the look in his eyes made her not want to argue.

The look in his eyes seemed to be saying something else entirely.

This was crazy. This was madness. This was the last thing they should be doing right now.

'So what normally happens on day four with John Carter, then?' Her words were whispered, the air rich with innuendo. 'Is he a fast mover?'

He moved a little closer, that look of cool amusement appearing across his face again. 'Well, day one might involve a little touching, a little stroking.' His voice was deep and husky and doing terrible things to her skin. 'Day two might involve something a little closer.' His fingers brushed along her shoulder blade. 'Maybe touching the neck or some sensitive skin.' His fingers picked up her thin silver chain, running downwards until he captured her delicate pendant in his fingers, brushing the skin above her breasts.

'What about day three?' Lily could barely get the words out.

His lips touched the top of her ear. 'Day three would definitely have involved some kissing,' he said with confidence, 'meaning that by day four things could have moved along entirely.'

His hand was resting at the back of her head. 'We seem to have missed a few steps,' she breathed.

'I guess we need to catch up, then,' he whispered as he pulled her head closer to his and touched his lips against hers. The effect was electric. This was no light touch. His lips instantly coaxed her mouth open. His fingers ran down her spine and his tongue eased into her mouth. There was a drive, an insistence behind it. She almost wished she had all her working body parts so could she change position and straddle him in the back of the taxi.

Her hands moved instantly, first on his chest then at the side of his face. She pulled his lips downwards, letting them find the delicate skin at the base of the throat, causing her to let out a little gasp.

He pulled backwards, the twinkle in his eye even brighter. 'So that's what you like,' he growled as he started to kiss her again, from behind one ear lobe down the stretch of her throat and round to the other side.

She was losing her mind. Last time she'd behaved like this in the back of cab she'd been around eighteen and on a strict curfew.

Her mind tried to focus. But she didn't want to. This felt too good to be interrupted by normal, rational thoughts.

Her hands swept downwards and then she felt it. Exactly what she was looking for. Something hard, pressing against her, looking for release. Now she really wished she could change position. This damn cast was nothing but a nuisance—in more ways than one.

She felt his sharp intake of breath. The release of his hands from her spine as he let her go. His hands had stopped touching her and she wanted to shout at him.

But she couldn't as his lips were still enfolding hers. He was still tasting her, still teasing her. His mouth tugged at her bottom lip as he pulled back from her, leaving her breathless and wanting in the back of the cab.

She sat back, pressing her shoulders against the black leather seat. She couldn't get any words out. Her stomach was churning. Was he embarrassed? Did he think he'd made a mistake?

With the jumbled thoughts spinning around in her

brain right now, she couldn't even begin to make sense of anything.

In the darkness his hand crept over and resumed its firm position on her thigh.

One word. 'Wow.'

Lily let out a slow breath of relief and a smile crept over her face. Not such a mistake after all.

CHAPTER FIVE

LILY stretched out in her bed like the proverbial cat that had got the cream. Bliss. Her eyes flickered to the digital clock. Nine a.m. She was getting truly and utterly lazy. She never slept this late. If she'd been on duty in the Western General they'd already be halfway through the first surgery of the day.

With a huge sigh she flung back the sheets and swung her legs out of bed. She'd been here nearly a week and was getting used to living in the lap of luxury. She was even getting proficient on her crutches.

She hobbled through to the kitchen and let out a laugh. The deluxe coffee maker was festooned in sticky notes, each consecutively numbered and some with instructions. All this after her 'incident' with the coffee maker the other morning. She smiled. Even when he wasn't here, he still managed to charm her.

She jumped as her phone beeped beside her. Remember to bring the paper in. C. She'd forgotten about the paper yesterday and Carter had picked it up from the sodden grass on his way in last night.

She wrestled with the front door and picked the paper up from the front porch. She wasn't even dressed yet and the cool morning air licked at her skin through her leopard print nightie. The sun was high in the clear sky—it would be a perfect day for a jump. Lily counted down the days in her head. Five weeks to go in a cast. Just as well Carter was proving such a distraction.

She closed the door behind her and leaned against it. It had been two days since he'd kissed her. Two long, long days.

When they'd got home that night, he'd brushed a kiss to her forehead and wished her goodnight. The next morning he'd brought her breakfast in bed and sat at the patio table talking to her as he'd eaten his. He hadn't seemed embarrassed. He hadn't seemed at all flustered. He'd been as cool as a cucumber and she found it strangely compelling.

The air between them sizzled. And every now and then she caught him looking at her with one of those long, lingering glances that made every hair on her arms stand on end. There was nothing platonic in those glances. But worse than that she didn't want there to be.

Then there had been that other near miss when she'd dropped a cup in the kitchen and he'd rushed to help her. His hands had brushed against hers as he'd picked up the broken shards, their heads bent close together. And again that pause, their lips only inches from each other. Space that could be covered in the blink of an eye. The breath had caught halfway in her throat as she'd waited to see what he would do next.

Then, a sexy smile as he'd brushed the jagged shards away from her and gathered them together in his hands, walking away towards the garbage pail.

And for her, the sharp feeling of disappointment. As if she'd just missed out on something important. If he didn't kiss her again soon she was going to die of frustration.

For the first time in a long time she'd met a man who could match her. Physically. Mentally. And definitely sexually. If only he didn't have imminent fatherhood in his plans.

Even at a push, a part-time father she could probably have coped with. But a full-time father? Under circumstances such as these? The involvement of courts and judges and interim orders? She'd heard him on the phone the other day to his attorney and then to the clinic.

It was apparently standard practice in circumstances such as these to seek an interim order so that when the baby was born, custody would be granted to him. The thought that there was 'standard practice' for these circumstances was mind-boggling to Lily. How often did that happen?

A search on the internet yesterday had revealed that this one-in-a-million case was much more common that she'd first imagined.

And it all came down to human error.

The thought absolutely appalled her and sent shivers down her spine. If she made a mistake at work, she could potentially kill someone. A wrong dose of drug, a missed note of an allergy, a missed symptom could result in something fatal. The most dangerous aspects of the job always required checks by two professionals. Even taking a patient to Theatre required it.

So how could something like this happen in a lab? How could they mislabel? How could they wrongly implant?

Then the other thought that had been circulating in her mind emerged. Were her eggs safe? Had they been mislabelled, lost or, even worse, wrongly implanted too?

Her hands went to the phone and she dialled the clinic number off by heart. 'I need an appointment to see Rhonda Fulton.' The picture of the woman floated in front of her eyes. Dark hair pulled back into a bun, red lipstick, glasses and a pinstriped suit. She'd never really liked the woman much.

'I'm sorry, Ms Fulton isn't taking appointments at the moment,' the smooth-voiced secretary answered.

Lily instantly felt her hackles rise. 'She'll see me.'

'Ms Fulton isn't seeing anyone. You'll just have to wait for the next press release,' came the sharp reply.

Lily felt herself seethe. The secretary obviously thought she was some press hack trying to bum her way into the clinic.

She gritted her teeth. 'Tell Ms Fulton that Lily Grayson, that would be Lily Grayson egg donor, needs to speak to her immediately. And give her my number.' She rattled off Carter's phone number.

The phone rang a few minutes later and Lily was almost tempted to let it go to voicemail. After the sixth ring she finally picked it up.

'Yes?'

'Ms Grayson?' came the Earl Grey tones. 'It's Rhonda Fulton here.'

'I thought you weren't taking calls?' Lily couldn't help herself. At this moment not only was she an egg donor, she was also a patient. She expected some professionalism from the clinic she dealt with. How many other panicked clients had phoned and been treated to the same response?

Rhonda cleared her throat. 'I'm not taking calls from press, Ms Grayson.'

'Well, I'm hardly the press, am I?'

'Of course not. How can I help you?'

Lily was astounded by her arrogance. Why on earth did she think she was calling? To chat about the weather?

She felt a cold veil come over her face. Normally, it

took a lot to annoy Lily, but this woman had managed it in a few seconds.

'First of all, Rhonda—' she emphasised the word heavily, hoping the familiarity would unseat the normally ice-cold woman '—I would like to know why the clinic did not have the professional courtesy to contact me over the recent revelations.'

The voice at the end of the phone wavered. 'And what revelations might those be?'

Lily was definitely ready to combust. 'The ones that are currently all over the press and the reason you're not taking any appointments right now. The ones that say that my donated egg was wrongly implanted in another woman.'

There was silence at the end of the line. Rhonda Fulton was obviously considering her next move. 'I don't know how you came about this information, Ms Grayson. However, you will remember that once you signed your eggs over to the clinic, complete anonymity was guaranteed. I can't comment on the recent press allegations…' She was gathering momentum, obviously catching her wind again and feeling confident in her spiel.

Lily sighed. 'Look at the telephone number, Rhonda. Do you recognise it at all?' She gave the woman a few moments to glance at her screen and see the number, and to allow the penny to drop. When she heard the sharp intake of breath she continued, 'John Carter contacted me last week. I may be anonymous to the press, but I was never anonymous to the people that selected me as their egg donor. My details were always available to them.'

She let her words sink in, hoping at some moment this smooth-talking woman would finally feel some of the shame that she should.

'In that case, Ms Grayson, I suggest you contact the clinic's attorneys as I feel it is inappropriate for us to have a discussion regarding any of the surrounding events.'

'I'm not finished with you yet, Ms Fulton.' Lily's voice was as cold as ice.

'Excuse me?'

'I will be talking to your attorneys—because Mr Carter has asked me to be his witness in court. But what I'd like from you first is an explanation as to why you didn't notify me in advance of this error. Then I want you to explain how an error like this can occur in your clinic. You assured me of your clinic's professionalism and expertise when I donated my eggs, and I'm appalled by the events. Finally, I want a written assurance from you that the eggs I currently have in storage with you are undamaged, correctly labelled and available for future use. After all, Ms Fulton, I am a patient of yours.' Her tones were clipped and self-assured. She wanted answers and she wanted them now.

She could almost swear she heard a hiss at the end of the phone. 'I can assure you,' came the obviously rattled voice at the end of the phone, 'that everything in the clinic is maintained to our high standards. Your eggs are still stored with us in perfect condition.'

'Since I'm not particularly impressed by your "high standards" right now, it won't surprise you to know that I may wish to see that for myself.'

Silence. Ms Fulton was obviously losing her patience. 'Of course.' The words sounded as if they had been spat out.

'I'll call at a later date. And I assume you'll be available to take my call?'

'Of course.'

'Good.' Lily hung up the phone and took a deep

breath. What had just come over her? She wouldn't normally speak to someone like that. Her heart was racing in her chest.

She limped outside and sat down on a patio chair, next to the pool. What she wouldn't give right now just to dive in and power up and down a few laps. Burn off some of this excess energy. She wrinkled her nose. Why hadn't they designed a cast for regular use that could easily get wet? She knew that in some cases people did get waterproof casts, but they were probably for the super-rich. And why did everyone still call them 'plasters' when they were made of fibreglass?

Her phone beeped again and she picked it up.

Have you blown up my coffee machine yet? C.

The message sent an instant smile across her face. She texted back.

Still trying, L.

In spite of his multitude of sticky notes, she'd already jammed a pod in the coffee machine that he'd need to prise out later.

What would he say when he found out about her call today? She hadn't told him about her own stored eggs. It hadn't seemed appropriate. And she wasn't entirely sure that she wanted to. She wasn't really ready to have that conversation about early menopause, depressed sisters and worrying about the future with a man she'd only kissed once. With a man she wasn't entirely sure of her feelings about. Particularly when she was contemplating how soon she could kiss him again...

She gave herself a shake and looked out over the

spacious back yard. Somewhere, in some part of San Francisco, another woman was sitting contemplating her future too. Another woman would be sitting with her hands resting on her bump, feeling a little baby moving under her skin and wondering what the hell had happened to her life.

Lily almost felt as if she could feel the baby move herself. How devastating. How heart-breaking. And this baby had developed a medical condition and required treatment. She couldn't even begin to imagine the strain this woman was under.

It would be bad enough to know something was wrong with your baby—but then to find out it wasn't your baby. It wasn't your husband's. It wasn't the one piece of hope that you'd clung to in widowhood. The tiny piece of hope that you'd had.

And in a matter of weeks you might have to hand over the little bundle you'd nursed inside you for nine months. The precious little bundle that had kept you awake at night.

Lily felt physically sick. Everything about this seemed so wrong. She knew the genetics. She knew this was her baby too. Maybe, in a lifetime far away, in a different world, she might even have considered what a child between her and Carter might look like, but right now she couldn't even contemplate it.

If she did, she might have to consider all the dark thoughts that were creeping around her brain. What if she did suffer from early menopause and needed to use her stored eggs to get pregnant?

Everyone knew there were no guarantees with IVF. The hard facts were that the odds were against you. Carter had already been through the emotional turmoil of IVF with his former wife.

His marriage hadn't survived it. Would another relationship fare any better?

And why should he even contemplate it? There was nothing wrong with him. He could go and father a whole baseball team of kids if he wanted—all the natural way. No clinics visits, no test tubes, no sample jars. Why would anyone put themselves through that if they didn't have to?

She shuddered. She didn't want to think about this. This was all just wild fairy-tales in her overactive imagination. Carter wasn't giving any of these things a moment's thought. He was concentrating on trying to win custody of his baby.

And as much as she was attracted to Carter—as much as she tried to understand his dilemma, his desire for a child, as much as she wanted to help him—something was burning deep in her stomach.

No matter how hard she tried, she just couldn't get her head around this. Deep down, her sympathies were with Olivia. Her position in all this was unimaginable. Lily couldn't help but wonder how her sister would have dealt with it, and what it would have done to her mental health.

Would she have come out the other side? Even thinking about it sent a shiver down her spine.

Then there was Carter, who was proving more than a little distracting. He may have contacted her in highly unusual circumstances, but the fact was she liked him. He was a good guy. He would be a good father. And her mixed-up attraction to him was in danger of influencing her behaviour.

And that, more than anything, frightened her. She was Lily Grayson. She always did exactly what she wanted. No one influenced her. No one made her change her mind about things. Self-assured and confident were two of the first words that her friends would use to describe her.

So why was she feeling uncomfortable? Why did all of this make her lose sleep at night? And why did a smile automatically appear on her face every time a text from Carter appeared?

Lily shivered, even though the Californian sun was shining, because for her this whole situation was getting out of control.

Carter looked at his page as it sounded for the fifth time. He was stuck in Theatre, his hands enclosed in surgical gloves and currently inside someone's hip joint. His theatre nurse had just dropped a whole set of instruments—she was obviously unnerved by the ever-insistent page too—and was currently unwrapping a clean set.

He signalled to the anaesthetist. 'Logan, can you grab that page from my pocket and tell me who's so impatient?'

Logan gave a nod and slid his hand under Carter's surgical gown and pulled the pager from his waistband. 'Call your attorney,' he said, raising his eyebrows. 'Must be baby stuff.' He switched the pager off and laid it down next to him.

Carter cringed. It irritated him that everyone knew what was happening—that everyone was whispering behind his back. His front-page headlines were the talk of the hospital. Everyone had an opinion on it. And all his colleagues looked at him in the corridor with sympathy in their eyes.

Carter bit his lip under his mask. Having his business splashed across the papers was infuriating. But he'd no one to blame but himself. It would be so much easier if he could pick up the phone and yell at the clinic's general manager for a breach of confidence, but the truth was it was his fault. He'd lost it when he'd got that letter. And after he'd made contact with his attorney to establish some of the facts, he'd ranted to some of his colleagues about how unbelievable it all was.

And, hospitals being hospitals, word had spread fast. He'd no idea who'd spoken to the press—whether it was deliberate or unwittingly—he'd just known that the route of the information had been via him.

A fact that had made him cringe when he'd realised he'd revealed Olivia's name. He really should apologise. He should explain that it was his fault and that he had done it out of frustration, not malice.

But he hadn't had opportunity to speak to Olivia. In fact, his attorney had advised there be no contact whatsoever. And to be honest, he was more comfortable with that.

Because Lily had started to get to him. She'd started to make him see this from the other side. He'd started to feel the horror creep over him that must have affected Olivia when she'd found out it wasn't her husband's baby and there was a possibility she wouldn't get to keep it.

And even though he tried not to think about it—to remain focused on the fact that this was his baby—the little prickles of doubt still rankled in his mind. The last thing he wanted to do was look into that woman's eyes and see exactly how she felt. It would probably be more than he could bear.

In the meantime, he could focus on his patient. A fit seventy-year-old who needed a new hip to keep up on the golf course. With luck, Mr Grant would be up and on his feet again within twenty-four hours, well on his way to recovery.

If only the same could be said for him.

* * *

Carter pulled the mask and gown from his body and shoved them in the nearest clinical waste bin. Three hours of theatre, followed by an emergency summons to the ER to help with an injured biker meant that he still hadn't followed up on that page.

He strode down the corridor to his office and closed the door behind him, taking a few seconds to lean against it and take some long deep breaths. He needed his head to be straight before he made this call. He couldn't afford distractions.

His smartphone beeped and he laughed at a photo sent by Lily. *Do you really have the oldest gardener in the world?* It showed Bill, his gardener, dressed in his usual baseball cap and joggers, pushing his wheelbarrow about the back yard with a stunned expression on his face. He'd forgotten to tell Lily about him. Another text followed. *And just when I'd decided it was safe to sunbathe topless...*

The words sent a rush of heat to his groin and an instant grin to his face. His fingers moved before his brain engaged. *I wish you'd sent me that photo instead. C.* She was distracting him. Again. But he welcomed it. It was if she was a constant undercurrent in his brain. Always there, just waiting to be unleashed.

He set his cellphone on the desk and rubbed his temples with his fingers. The headache that had started as mild this morning in Theatre was beginning to build to a crescendo. And needless to say he had no painkillers in his desk.

He picked up his work phone and dialled the number for his attorney. The phone was answered in seconds by the efficient PA. 'It's John Carter. Is Cole available?'

'Right away, Mr Carter.'

He waited a few seconds until Cole came on the line. 'Carter, where have you been?'

'In surgery, Cole. I'm a surgeon, that's where they pay me to be. What's wrong?' His heart started to thud in his chest. Cole sounded panicked. Was something wrong with the baby?

'I've got those details you wanted, and they might cause us a problem in court.'

'What details?' Carter tried to focus. They'd discussed a million different things and this could be any one of a dozen.

'You asked about Olivia's embryos. It turns out the mislabelling caused her samples to be destroyed instead of yours.'

Carter felt his stomach drop. That was it. She'd lost her chance to have her husband's child. As if being implanted with the wrong embryo wasn't enough to deal with.

He kept his voice steady. 'How does this influence our case, Cole?'

Cole was a brilliant attorney. He could ferret information out of anywhere and he'd spent the last two weeks pulling information from dozens of other cases across the U.S. in order to give them the best chance of success. He didn't believe in beating around the bush. 'It's the sympathy vote, Carter. It's bad enough that she's a widow. But this is just the icing on the cake. She's lost part of her husband through a clinical error. And although we'll never know if any of those embryos would have implanted successfully, now she'll never have the chance to find out.'

Carter heard him suck in a deep breath. Cole didn't really do sympathy. He didn't really do the human angle.

But he was obviously giving careful consideration to everything right now.

Focus. That's what he had to do right now. 'So what can we do about it?'

'Right now? Nothing. Our one positive note is that the woman is fertile. They only went down the IVF route because of her husband's illness. With any luck she could meet someone else and go on to have a family with him.'

Carter swallowed the words that came instantly to his lips. He was appalled. This was life they were talking about. This was a baby. A real, live soon-to-be-here person. Not some doll. Not some item.

He wanted to explode, to erupt at Cole over his devil-may-care attitude. He wanted to shout at Cole that that would be little, or possibly no, consolation to Olivia right now. But Cole was working for him. Cole was looking out for his best interests. Cole was trying to gain him custody of his child.

This wasn't emotional for Cole, it was purely work. And that was just as well. He could see things much more clearly than Carter could.

'What about Lily?'

'What about Lily?' Carter frowned. Where was this going?

'Have you talked to her yet? Is she willing to appear in court? You know, you really need to get her to come and see me. I need to brief her. I need to make sure she says exactly what we want her to.'

Carter could feel the hackles go up at the back of his neck. He wasn't sure how he felt about that.

He'd tracked Lily down for the simple reason of helping his case. But the lines had started to blur now. He knew instantly that Lily wouldn't be told what to say or do.

That was one of the things he liked about her.

He also knew that a woman who'd sold her eggs and had a list of wild pastimes probably wouldn't be the best to help his case. He could already sense that Cole would want her to change her appearance, her clothes and probably lie about how she'd injured her ankle. And he wasn't sure he felt entirely comfortable with that.

Maybe he needed to sleep on it?

'You'll need to give me a little more time with Lily,' he said briskly.

'A little more time to lay on the Carter charm?' Cole's voice was thick with innuendo, instantly causing his temper to flare.

'Leave it, Cole. Let me deal with Lily.'

But Cole cut him off. 'No, Carter. That's my job. And if you want to win custody of your baby, you're going to have to let me deal with Lily.' His voice was firm.

Carter put the phone down. He knew that Cole was right, but nothing made sense right now. This whole screwed-up scenario—meeting Lily, and his imminent unexpected fatherhood all continued to circulate around his brain in ever-decreasing circles.

He'd already monumentally messed up one relationship by wanting children. He'd been so intent on creating his perfect family he hadn't even seen the effect it had been having on Tabitha. And although there had been faults on both sides, in hindsight he realised he hadn't given her the support and understanding she'd deserved. And now it seemed as if he was speeding down the highway intent on sabotaging another relationship.

Because all of a sudden that's what this was—a relationship. Lily featured in his every waking thought. The original plan of having her help him in court seemed to be fading more gradually into the distance with every day that passed. Maybe he should just leave Lily out of all this?

He glanced at his watch. Nearly five p.m. On a normal day, he never left the hospital before seven. But today wasn't normal. He'd have a quick check of his post-op patients, then hand over to the on-call doc.

Thirty minutes later he was done and headed out to the car park, helmet in hand, ready to go home. As usual, he had nothing in the fridge for dinner, so decided to duck into the nearby store for some food.

He jammed his basket with chicken, chillies, salad and dessert. There was a woman front of him in the queue with a baby and two toddlers, juggling her basket and purse and trying to keep hold of her kids.

'Here, let me.' Carter put down his basket and held out his hands for the baby.

The woman didn't think twice, 'Oh, thanks. I really need to have two sets of hands instead of one.' She handed over her baby and the two wrist straps for the toddlers while she bagged and paid for her purchases.

Carter knelt down, talking to the two toddlers while resting the baby on his knee. Three little boys. The twins looked just over two and the baby around six months. All were chubby, happy-looking kids. 'What are your names?' Carter asked as the twins stared at him.

'Louis,' mumbled the first one.

'Ben,' said the second, before he started rummaging through a shelf of candies near the checkout.

Carter bounced the baby on his knee. 'And what about you, little fella?'

'That's Arfur,' said Ben, as he shoved a chocolate bar, which he'd mysteriously unwrapped in two seconds flat, into his mouth.

Carter struggled to hide his laugh. 'You speak really

well, Ben. You must be...' he paused, pretending to think about it '...at least five years old.'

Ben was obviously impressed by the compliment. 'I'm two,' he shouted, a smile spreading across his face.

Arthur decided to wrap his chubby hands around Carter's neck, with inevitable drool landing on his shoulder. Louis, in the meantime, had decided to sit down on the floor and unfasten his shoes.

Carter sat in amazement as an air of complete contentment swept over him. This was exactly what he wanted. The chaos of three kids seemed entirely alien to some people, but not to him. The joy of waking up in the morning to a family, a house filled with knees covered in sticky plasters and, as he watched Louis stuff one of his shoes under the cash desk, a frantic twenty-minute hunt every morning for a missing shoe. He couldn't think of a single thing he wanted more.

Except Lily.

He shook off the thought as soon as it came.

The woman at the cash desk finished her packing and turned around with a broad smile and outstretched arms. 'Thank you so much for that. Come on, little guy.' Arthur let out a shriek of excitement and leaned back towards his mother.

'My pleasure,' said Carter quietly, sliding the wrist straps back onto her arm. He bent down and retrieved Louis's missing shoe from under the counter, pulling back the Velcro and fastening it back onto his foot.

'Oh, wow, thanks. I would have missed that.' The woman smiled. 'I need eyes in the back of my head. You're a natural at this, I bet you've got a baseball team of kids at home.' She smiled down at her twins. 'Let's go, guys,' she said, tugging at the wrist straps and leading them out of the store.

Carter felt his breath catch in his throat. He didn't even notice the cashier ring through his items and brown bag them for him. He was too frozen in the moment. He felt as if a weight was pressing down on his chest.

Why did it matter what the stranger thought? Why did it matter that she assumed he was a father and thought he was a natural with kids?

He must have heard words like these a thousand times throughout his lifetime. From friends, colleagues, work-mates and strangers he'd met on occasion and inter-acted with their kids. He'd always laughed and joked with them.

Even when Tabitha had been going through IVF and they had been desperate for a child, he'd still managed to be casual in his responses.

So what was wrong with him? Why did he feel like this now?

'Sir? Excuse me, sir? That'll be eighteen dollars.'

'What? Oh, sorry.' Carter pulled some cash out from his pocket, paid and grabbed the brown bag. He crammed it into the front of his leather jacket, before pulling his helmet back on and swinging his leg over the bike.

He gunned the bike through the back streets of San Francisco, hugging the corners on the ten-minute journey to his home. It was a gorgeous, mild evening. A perfect evening to spend with a beautiful woman.

But Carter's stomach was churning with unease. He felt uncomfortable. This couldn't go on much longer.

Lily was sitting nervously on the comfortable sofa, the front windows open, listening for the inevitable sound from the road.

For the last half-hour she'd expected to him appear at any minute. And then she heard it, the roar of the engine as he pulled up outside. She struggled to her feet, grabbing her crutches and pulling the front door open.

Carter strode down the path with purpose, pulling his helmet from his head in one easy movement. She stared at him. His blue eyes were focused, a light sheen of sweat on his brow.

They spoke at the same time.

'We need to talk.'

CHAPTER SIX

CARTER woke early from one of the worst night's sleeps he'd ever had. He rubbed the sleep from his eyes and pulled back the curtains. The blue pool was glistening in the early morning light and it took less than ten seconds to make up his mind on how to start the day.

He powered up and down the pool, lap after lap, burning away the restless energy that had kept him awake all night. His muscles responded automatically, almost as if they were anxious to have a purpose. He kept his face down in the cool water, turning sideways to suck air into his burning lungs. The tension finally started to loosen across his shoulders and back.

Nothing had gone well last night. He'd been snappy and frustrated. Lily had appeared agitated and unsure of anything. They'd talked themselves around in circles and achieved nothing, both stomping off to bed around midnight.

It hadn't helped that no matter how much they couldn't agree on anything, there was a permanent undercurrent sizzling between them. Every touch, no matter how fleeting, seemed to send fireworks scattering between them.

Carter pulled himself from the pool and grabbed his towel, drying his hair as he walked through the house to the front door. For once his paperboy seemed to have made it out of bed on time as the paper lay waiting on the porch. He tucked it under his arm and headed for kitchen.

He inserted a pod and flicked the button on the coffee machine, lifting the griddle pan and pulling a jug of pancake batter from the fridge. Making breakfast for Lily would surely get the day off to a better start.

He busied himself as the pancakes started to sizzle, flipping some bacon and watching the coffee start to drizzle into the nearby cups, followed by frothed and steamed milk. Another couple of minutes and everything would be ready. Perfect.

He unfolded the paper. There were a couple of smudges from where he'd tucked it under his damp arm, so it took him a few seconds to realise what he staring at.

He grabbed it closer, staring at the coloured picture on the front page, his breath catching in his chest. Lily. It was definitely Lily.

Dressed only in her very short leopard print nightie and leaning forward to pick up the newspaper, giving a clear and ample shot of her cleavage. In front of his house.

He froze. The headline was the sucker punch: 'Doc Moves in Egg Donor in Bid to Win Custody of Mix-Up Baby'.

No!

Rage circulated around him. How on earth had they got that photograph? How did they know who Lily was? He racked his brain. He might have slipped up when he'd found out about the mistaken implantation—but he was sure he hadn't told anyone about Lily. Only his attorney knew about Lily. He cringed. But who had Lily spoken to? She must have spoken to some family or friends— maybe they had revealed who she was?

Pancakes and bacon forgotten, he strode through the house and flung open the door to Lily's room.

Lily jumped. She'd been having the most blissful dream, filled with beautiful sandy beaches, exotic cocktails and long passionate kisses—but it certainly hadn't ended like this. Carter stood in the doorway wearing only a pair of swimming shorts, water still dripping from some parts of his bare, flat chest. Maybe this was still part of the dream?

But—no. A towel was thrown over his shoulder and it was clear that he'd just slammed the door off the wall. He looked furious and was clutching something in his hand. His blue eyes were almost black, the tight clench of his jaw making her sit upright in bed and pull the covers around her to hide her bare skin. This wasn't a happy visit.

Her sleep-addled brain tried to pull her into the here and now. Although things had been tense between them last night, as far as she could remember, they'd both gone their separate ways to bed. She was absolutely sure that she'd spent the last eight hours sleeping. How on earth could she have upset him?

Carter strode over to her bed and flung something at her. 'Where the hell did they get this picture? Who did you tell you were here?'

Lily felt her hackles rise, putting her on the defensive. She didn't like to be on the back foot. She liked to be prepared for things.

She picked up the crumpled newspaper, scanning it quickly before letting her jaw hang open at the semi-naked photo of herself. 'What...?'

Her eyes fell downwards. She'd slept naked last night because her nightie was currently in the washing basket. The nightie she'd been wearing yesterday morning. The nightie she was wearing in that picture. 'You can practically see my—'

'I can see that,' he snapped. 'In fact, I think the whole world can see that.'

Lily felt the colour flush into her cheeks. She started to read the text, biting the inside of her cheek as she read the headline. Her heart started to thud in her chest as she took rapid, shorter breaths. This was a disaster.

She got to the end and flung the newspaper away in disgust.

'Well?' He was standing at the end of the bed with his hands on his hips. Although the steam was practically coming out of his ears, Lily could see the irony in all this. Particularly when he was wearing so little.

She folded her arms across her chest. 'I'm not happy about being splashed across a newspaper, Carter. But do you want to explain exactly why you're angry with me?'

'What?'

She rolled her eyes. 'Can we only speak in words of one syllable?'

His brow furrowed.

'Well? What? Is that all you can say?'

'Who did you tell? Who did you tell that you were staying here? People have seen the headlines. Did your workmates know you were an egg donor? Have you told someone, or did they put two and two together?'

'Whoa, John!' Lily held her hands up, completely oblivious to the fact that the sheet was sliding downwards. 'Hold it right there.'

He'd started pacing around the room. Under ordinary circumstances she might have been quite happy to sit back and admire the view, but nothing about this situation was normal.

Her stomach was churning. She didn't know what was upsetting her more—the fact she was splashed across the newspaper or the fact that Carter thought she'd something to do with it.

He turned back to face her. 'How on earth did they get that picture? When did they take it? And why on earth would you go to the front door looking like that?' He froze, noticing the fact that her sheet had slid down her body, revealing one pink-tipped breast.

'Why on earth would you go to the front door looking like that?' She pointed to his bare chest and swim shorts. 'Or do you get fully dressed every morning in case there's some hack photographer at your front door?'

Carter was still staring at her and it took her a few seconds to realise what he was looking at. Lily looked downwards, rolled her eyes and pulled the sheet up, completely unembarrassed. She swung her legs to the edge of the bed and wrapped the sheet around her as best she could.

'Do you know what? I don't even want to be here. I don't even know if I'm going to help you yet. And the last thing I want is my private business spread all over the local news. I haven't told anyone at work what I did in the past. I'm not happy about them knowing now.' She pointed to her chest. 'To them I'm Lily Grayson, theatre nurse, and a damn good one at that. I don't want them to know me as Lily Grayson, egg donor. I don't want them wondering why I did it. That part of my life is mine— private. And it's no one else's business. At least it wasn't until you flung me into the middle of all this.'

Carter's face paled and his anger started to ebb. Two little red spots had appeared on Lily's cheeks. No matter how angry he was right now, he couldn't ignore the fact that she was right. She hadn't asked for any of this.

He stared down at his bare chest. He'd picked up the

paper from the porch this morning without a second thought about what he was—or was not—wearing. Why should Lily be any different?

The smell of smoke drifted down the corridor. Carter bolted back to the kitchen to scrape the black remnants of pancakes and bacon from the stove.

He sighed. So much for starting the day off well. He walked back into the bedroom. Lily hadn't moved, but before he could start to speak the air was shattered by the ringing of the phone. Neither of them moved and a few seconds later the answering-machine kicked in. 'This is Frank Brewster from the *Gazette*, I wonder if we could have a quote...'

They cringed, waiting for the message to click off.

He stepped over and sank down on the bed next to her. 'I'm sorry,' he murmured. 'I guess I'm not thinking straight right now.' He couldn't meet her gaze. He couldn't look at that pale skin wrapped in the white sheet.

Lily's voice quietened. 'In case you haven't noticed, John...' she lifted her leg encased in the purple cast '...I haven't been at work for nearly two weeks. I haven't been in touch with my workmates. So none of them could have spoken to the press.' Her brow wrinkled. 'What about the last story—how did the press get hold of that?'

Carter cringed. 'Yeah, about that...'

'What?'

He blew out a long hiss of air through his lips. 'That might have been my fault.'

'Tell me you're joking?'

He ran his fingers through his dark hair. 'I wish I was.' He turned to face her and for the first time she noticed tiny worry lines around his eyes. 'When I found out about the embryo being wrongly implanted I sort of blew up. I had a bit of a rant at work. I've no idea if someone spoke to the press—but logic tells me it wasn't Olivia or any of her friends. So I'm kind of assuming it was one of mine.'

She shook her head. 'And yet you come in here, all guns blazing, ready to read me the Riot Act?'

'I feel terrible about it.' He rolled his eyes. 'You have no idea what I said to the clinic's general manager—I assumed the leak had come from there.'

Lily gave him a rueful smile. 'Just tell me you didn't apologise to that woman.'

'Rhonda Fulton? Not a chance. But it didn't even strike me until I'd spoken to her that I could have caused the leak myself. I'm still not sure where it came from. And I've no idea where they got their latest update.'

Lily fingered the newspaper still lying on the bed. 'I guess it wouldn't be too difficult to find out who I am.' She shrugged her shoulders. 'Think about it. Anyone registered at the clinic that's looking for an egg donor has access to that database. And the way Rhonda Fulton has been speaking to her clients recently, it doesn't surprise me that someone went public.' She sighed.

'But this was at your expense. I'm so sorry, Lily. I guess I wasn't thinking about this from your point of view.'

'You're not too good at that, are you?'

There was a heaviness to her words, as if she'd resigned herself to the fact that, right now, Carter's only priority was getting custody of his baby. And anything that had been simmering between them was about to turn to dust.

He had the good grace to look shamefaced as the two of them sat in silence for a few moments, contemplating what to do next.

'You know what annoys me most about this, Carter?'

Lily was whispering, her voice raspy.

'What?' He lifted his hooded lids to her face. Scrubbed clean of make-up and with her natural green eyes she was beautiful. He was sitting on the bed with a beautiful woman he'd just shouted at. A woman who kept distracting him from his priorities.

She reached over and touched his arm with her fingertip. It was like someone had just turned on an electric current and sent it spiralling up his arm. 'This,' she said.

There was silence. The air hung heavily between them. Too much to say, and no words to say it.

She looked out across the garden. 'If I believe everything that's in the newspaper, then you'll do anything to persuade me to help. You'll do anything to win your case and get custody of your child.'

Her hand clutched at the sheet around her and he heard her sharp intake of breath. 'I just wonder what your anything entails.'

'You can't mean that.' The words shot out from his mouth automatically. 'You can't honestly think that.' He shook his head, trying to rid himself of the premise of that idea. His hand reached out for hers. He slid his broad palm over hers, encapsulating her hand in his. 'I could never do that, Lily.' His thumb started to trace little circles on the back of her hand. 'You can't fake this. Whatever this is between us, I could never fake that—I can't even explain it. I don't even know what it is.'

Lily bit her bottom lip. There was a lump in her throat the size of a tennis ball. A single tear slid down her cheek. 'But what if you did, John? What if that's all this is about? You keeping me onside. Helping you win your custody case.' She could feel her voice tremble. These thoughts had been lingering in the back of her brain, never fully formed, for days. Ever since he'd kissed her.

She was used to being sure. To being confident about everything. But John Carter had made her mind spin.

He gave her a rueful smile. 'I can't pretend I don't want your help, Lily.'

She tried to stand, grasping for her crutch with one hand and straightening in front of him. 'I wish I hadn't met you like this.' Her eyes were glistening, threatening to spill with more tears. She pointed at her cast. 'I wish I'd met you on a normal day, in a normal way, with none of this other stuff happening. I can't detach myself from all this. I can't detach myself from how all this makes me feel.'

He stood up in front of her and placed his hands on her bare shoulders. His fingers touched the small blonde strands of hair at the back of her neck. His eyes were fixed on hers, staring right at her, deep inside her. She felt herself move her head, tipping it backwards as his fingers ran through her hair, luxuriating in his touch. He took a step closer. The dark hairs on his chest came into contact with her electrified skin.

'I wish I'd met you under other circumstances too because I don't know how to make sense of all this. All I know is when I'm not with you it drives me crazy. I spend the whole time thinking about what I'll do when I see you again and…' he lowered his mouth to her ear '…I can't detach myself from how you make me feel.'

Lily felt off balance. And it was nothing to do with her cast or crutches. Her head was swimming. His words sent involuntary shivers down her spine. But…she liked it. The dark hairs on his chest were tickling the sensitive skin next to her breasts. Her eyes followed its trail downwards. Down past his lean brown muscles and flat abdomen. Down to where the tell-tale bulge in his swimming shorts was evident. All the message she needed.

An automatic smile played across her lips as she leaned forward, pressing herself against him. This was madness. All of the circumstances surrounding this were wrong. But Lily couldn't bear not to act on the heat between them. She had to know. She had to know if this was real or not.

Because right now she needed him. And not just in the physical sense—in the emotional sense too. She wanted to comfort him, to touch him and have him touch her and hold her as if they were meant to be together. As if they were meant to be doing this.

He moved his hand from her shoulders, starting at her wrist and tracing his finger up her arm. The lightest, the most delicate of touches that spelled a whole realm of possibilities. She looked up at him. Those blue eyes were totally fixed on her. The slight stubble on his chin intrigued her. Where exactly would she like to feel that stubble abrading her skin? The thoughts exploded in her head and almost instantly her hand released the Egyptian cotton sheet she was holding around her. It fell to the floor in a white puddle.

His reaction was instantaneous, his pupils dilating, the blackness almost obliterating his blue irises. She felt his eyes sweep down her body and revelled in it. Lily had never been ashamed of her body. His hands ran down her back, tracing the outline of her spine, feeling the swell of her hips, cupping her buttocks and pulling her hard against him.

'Tell me now, Lily, if you're sure about this,' he whispered in her ear, his voice thick with desire.

She could feel his hardness pressing next to her bare skin. Her legs felt as if they could buckle underneath her. There wasn't a single doubt in her mind. This was exactly what she wanted.

She wound her hands around his neck, 'Oh, I'm sure.'

Seconds later, Carter moved swiftly, sweeping his hand under her legs and laying her down on the white bed. He positioned himself above her, hands on either side of her head.

Lily lifted her hands and danced her fingers down his chest, watching with pleasure as he sucked in his stomach muscles. She slid her hands down the front of his shorts, wrapped herself around him, watching the expression on his face. She ran her fingers along his length, reaching down and cupping his balls. He let out an involuntary groan and Lily relished the feeling of being in control.

'I think you're a bit overdressed for the occasion,' she murmured. 'How am I supposed to get access to the bits of you I want?' she whispered, then laughed as he wasted no time in disposing of his shorts.

He pressed his full body weight against hers, skin against skin, his thick erection nudging her abdomen. 'How's this?'

Lily arched her back, pushing her body even closer to his. 'Oh, that's much better,' she breathed. 'You're definitely moving in the right direction now.' Lily opened her legs, anchoring them around his hips.

He raised his eyebrows at her. 'What's the hurry, Ms Grayson? I think we've got all day. Why rush things?'

The words made her stomach coil in anticipation. This wasn't to be some quick heat-of-the-moment passion. This was to be a leisurely stroll in the park. The very thought made her skin tingle.

He started kissing under her ear, his trail coming around the front of her neck and down towards her breasts. Her nipples were peaking, waiting for his attention, urging him to notice them, and she groaned, feeling the stubble graze her skin. She tried to move herself, edging her nipple closer to his mouth.

'Patience, Ms Grayson,' he growled as he came back up and started kissing around the back of the other ear.

She moved again, brushing the tips of her hardened nipples against his broad chest, watching the expression on his face.

Her body was on fire. She didn't want to wait. She didn't want to have patience. She could feel the liquid heat between her legs. She wanted to feel him nudging against her. She tried to put her hands down between their bodies again, but he caught them and pushed them back on either side of her head.

'I don't want to wait.' Her words were loud and clear and she stared straight into his eyes. 'Now, Carter,' she urged.

He paused just for a second, then opened the bottom drawer in the cabinet next to the bed.

In his unbalanced position Lily used the opportunity to push at his chest, flipping him over onto his back. She pulled the silver wrapper from his hand, grinning. 'Let me.' She tore open the packet and watched his face contort as she rolled the sheath down his hard length. She winked at him. 'Cheeky rascal—did you think your luck was in?' She positioned herself above him.

He grabbed her hips and lowered her. 'Let's just not look at the best-before date.' He smiled as he filled her and she let out a gasp.

Lily moved her hips, adjusting for the stretch, and leaned forward, brushing her nipples against his chest. 'Now, what did you say about having all day…?'

Carter woke up to the doorbell ringing and a loud, insistent knock at the door. He pulled on a T-shirt and shorts and took a few seconds to peer through the peephole, checking for journalists—the events of the last few days had made him nervous.

No one there.

Except the knock on the door was continuing.

He opened the door and looked down. 'Hey, Carter.' The small seven-year-old shouldered his way through the gap in the door, swimsuit in one hand and a baseball glove in the other. 'It's Saturday,' he said simply, as if that were all the explanation Carter needed.

Carter smiled. 'Hey, Donovan.' He glanced over his shoulder at the clock on the wall. Eight a.m. 'Did someone throw you out of bed this morning?' He ruffled the little guy's hair. 'And where's your baseball cap? It's going to be a roaster today.'

Donovan wrinkled his nose. 'What's that smell?' He turned to face Carter. 'Did you buy flowers?' For a seven-year-old, he looked suitably aghast.

Carter sniffed the air. And then his T-shirt—which had a distinct smell of Lily's honeysuckle perfume. He sighed. 'I've got a girl staying—it must be her. When you get older, you'll realise all girls smell like that.'

He walked into the kitchen. 'Have you had breakfast yet? Want some pancakes?' Second day in a row—maybe today's would be more successful.

Donovan nodded and wandered off in the other direction. 'Breakfast was hours ago,' he sighed. 'Pancakes would be cool.'

Lily opened her eyes and nearly leapt a foot in the air. 'Aargh!!' There was a small boy perched on the end of her bed, rubbing her moisturiser on his face.

'Hey.' He smiled at her, a big blob of cream falling off his nose and landing on the bed. He pointed at her body. 'You really should wear jammies in bed. I can see your boobies.'

Lily pulled up the sheet, horrified at some strange child seeing her naked body. 'Who are you?' she asked.

'I'm Donovan.'

She waited. And waited. Hoping for some other nugget of information. But Donovan ignored her, starting to rub her expensive moisturiser into his shins.

'Donovan who?'

The big brown eyes turned to face her again, as if he'd almost forgotten she was there. 'Donovan Marley. From across the street. It's Saturday,' he said, as if that was the answer to everything. He pointed out the patio doors to the swimming pool. 'We swim in Carter's pool on Saturdays—or play ball.' He picked up his baseball mitt. 'See?'

Lily's nose started to twitch. She could smell the warm aroma of pancakes floating down the hall towards her. Her brain began to focus. 'So, did Carter let you in?'

'Sure did. He's making pancakes. There better be syrup.' Donovan rolled his eyes, 'He never shops, you know.'

Lily nodded. 'Can you pass me that purple T-shirt, please?' she said.

Donovan jumped off the bed and picked up the T-shirt, wandering up to the top of the bed and staring at her closely.

'Carter said he had a girl staying.' He leaned forward and whispered conspiratorially in her ear, 'But you can't be his girlfriend, because you're sleeping in the spare bedroom.' He stood up straight, very pleased with himself for sharing his inside information.

Lily resisted the temptation to smile, pretending to

narrow her eyes. 'Why? Where does his girlfriend get to sleep?'

Donovan nodded his head in the other direction. 'Oh, the girlfriend gets to sleep in Carter's room.' He whispered again, 'But I haven't seen a girlfriend in a long time.' He tapped the side of his nose, obviously imitating the gesture seen from an adult. 'I've got three girlfriends right now. Carter doesn't seem to do too well with the girls.'

Lily pulled the T-shirt over her head, thankful it would almost reach her knees, and swung her legs out of the bed. 'You seem to know everything, Donovan.'

'Cool!' came the shout. 'You've got a cast and it's purple!' The mini-adult was lost and the little boy started jumping up and down. 'How did you get it? How did you get it?'

Lily tapped the side of her nose. 'I'll tell you—but you have to keep it a secret, okay?'

Donovan nodded furiously.

'I jumped out of a plane.'

'You did?' Donovan's eyes were as wide as saucers. 'Did you have a parachute?'

Lily nodded slowly, grabbing her crutches and standing up. 'I did, but it was broken. That's why I hurt my leg.'

'Did Carter fix it for you? Did he give you the purple cast? Can I have one too?'

Lily laughed at the explosion of questions.

'What's going on in here?'

The deep voice made them both jump. Carter was poised in the doorway with an amused expression on his face. He strode into the room and picked up Donovan. 'Come on, little guy, what about these pancakes?' Donovan nodded and smiled as Carter headed for the door. He turned and winked at Lily, his eyes roaming the length of her body. 'If madam is appropriately dressed, I've made some pancakes for her too.'

Lily smiled and grabbed her other crutch, limping after them down the hall.

This was going to be an interesting day.

CHAPTER SEVEN

TEN messages.

Lily peered at the display on Carter's house phone, a new-fangled thing that gave information on all the callers. She sighed. The *Gazette*. The *Courier*. The *Daily News*. Four TV stations and two gossip magazines.

No point even listening to them. Lily pressed delete.

Three days on and the newshounds still wouldn't leave them alone. At some point today one of them was bound to appear on the doorstep. She'd had to threaten yesterday's persistent caller with the garden hose before they'd finally left.

Her phone beeped. How many this morning? C x.

She pressed the buttons in rapid response. 10. L x.

The kisses had started to appear the morning after they'd slept together. And for a girl who didn't usually do outward signs of affection she kind of liked it.

A few seconds later the phone beeped again. I've got a surprise for you. See you in 5. C x

Lily felt a little tingle of pleasure run down her spine. What did that mean? She glanced at her watch—it was just after ten a.m. so Carter should be at work. What on earth was he doing? A smile crept across her face. Was he just sneaking home for some play time?

There had been no stopping him this last week, which

was just as well because she couldn't get enough of him. She loved the feel of his hands on her skin, his stubble scraping her cheek and the scent of him lingering on the sheets on her bed. Maybe she should be worried that they'd never made it through to his room—the master suite. But truth be told, she didn't care. She only wished her cast was off, then they could try out the swimming pool, her wet room, the Jacuzzi in his bathroom, all while wrapped around each other. Now she couldn't wipe the smile from her face. Maybe would she have to think more adventurously…

Lily jumped as there was a huge bang outside. It almost sounded like an explosion. 'What on earth…?' She grabbed her crutches—it was remarkable how quickly she could move now—and rushed to pull open the door.

Wow.

One of the streetlights was skewed at a peculiar angle, a car hood venting steam, crumpled at its base.

She was there in a few seconds, a quick look revealing only one person in the car. She flung her crutches aside and tugged with all her might at the dented driver's door. 'Y— Argh!' Finally it gave way, the momentous tug sending her reeling backwards and almost off her one steady foot.

She ignored the crutches and hopped forward, bending to look inside the car. It was one of Carter's neighbours, a middle-aged man, who lay slumped in the driver's seat. The airbag had thankfully deployed, with the tell-tale signs of minor abrasions on his face, and he was unconscious.

Lily stuck her fingers in at the side of his neck, trying to find the carotid pulse. Nothing. She took another few seconds, trying again at the other side of his neck, bending her head towards his mouth and listening, watching for the rise and fall of his chest. Again nothing. No pulse. No breathing.

She looked over her shoulder. Surely someone would come to help? Someone else must have heard the noise?

But the street was clear. She already knew that most of the residents worked and would have left for work a few hours ago. Her only hope was that one of the moms would return from making the school run—no yellow school bus for the kids in this area. There was nothing else for it. She would have to do it herself.

Her heart started fluttering in her chest. It had been a long time since Lily had been a first responder. Although many of the emergency cases in Theatre were unstable, by the time she saw them they had IV access, a cardiac monitor in place and an airway established. Not like now.

She pulled her phone from her back pocket and dialled 911, pressing the button for speakerphone and setting it on the dashboard as she tried to wedge her shoulder behind the driver and circle her arms around his torso.

Lily knew about neck injuries. She'd heard all the horror stories of people who'd been moved at the scene of an accident when they should have been left for the experts to deal with. But she had to prioritise. Her patient wasn't breathing and currently had no pulse.

'Nine-one-one, Eemergency.'

'I need an ambulance.' She cringed; she hadn't even given the dispatcher a chance to speak properly. She took a deep breath and heaved. Nothing. He was heavier than he looked. Lily tried to wedge herself further behind him to try and help edge him out of the driver's seat. This would be so much easier if she had two good legs.

'What is the nature of your emergency?'

'RTA, one unconscious male. No breathing. No pulse,' she shouted.

'Can you give me your name and your location?'

Lily rattled off her name and Carter's address. She gritted her teeth again and pulled. 'Oof!' Her adrenaline must have been pumping as his body edged towards her. She took another deep breath. 'Aargh.' She pulled the man from his seat but fell over, landing on the road, with him on top of her, his legs still caught in the car.

'Ms Grayson, are you okay? We'll have paramedics with you in five minutes.'

Lily scrambled from underneath the man, the wind knocked from her lungs. She pulled his legs free, leaving him positioned flat on the ground in front of her.

For a second she froze, glancing at the steam rising from the hood. Could she smell gas? No. In an ideal world she'd pull him away from the car before she commenced CPR but in an ideal world she'd have two good legs, and the reality was that she couldn't drag him away with one leg in a cast.

The voice cut through her thoughts. 'Ms Grayson, you said he's not breathing. Do you need some instructions on what to do next?'

Lily snapped out her stupor. 'No, I'm an RN. I know what to do. But I don't have any equipment and I'm on my own. Tell the paramedics to hurry.'

She positioned herself on her knees at the side of the patient, quickly checking his airway was clear before positioning her hands to begin chest compressions. She leaned forward, establishing the rhythm in her head, the tune of the Bee Gees playing 'Stayin' Alive' giving her the beat as she carried out her thirty compressions.

The irony of the tune, recommended by the American Heart Association, to help pace compressions appropriately wasn't lost on her.

She finished and tilted his head backwards, giving two long breaths before starting compressions again.

She tried to shift her position. Already her shoulders were beginning to burn, the cast proving troublesome, and she could feel the gravel on the road abrading her knees. Normally her toes would have been bent, to help anchor her to the ground and maintain her position. But with the cast on one foot, her position wasn't ideal.

Right now she'd kill for a bag and mask and a defibrillator. She'd no idea what rhythm his heart was in—all cardiac arrests in the hospital were quickly attached to a monitor, showing the heart rhythm and allowing hospital staff to follow the appropriate algorithm for treatment. A cannula and epinephrine would be handy too. She had to stop thinking like a hospital nurse.

She gave a quick glance around her. Still no one in sight. She placed her hands on his chest again and recommenced compressions, counting in her head while keeping to the beat of the song.

Five minutes. That's what the dispatcher had said. And five minutes was nothing. What could you do in five minutes? Make a pot of coffee. Make a sandwich. Put on some make-up. Change clothes.

Her arms were starting to feel the strain. She normally considered herself to be fit, taking part in keep-fit classes and kick-boxing every week, but this short spell of cardiac massage was making her feel like an old woman. She gritted her teeth and kept going. She was sure she could hear the dispatcher calling to her from the phone, but right now she didn't have the breath to answer. She needed to save all her breath for this. She leaned forward and pressed her mouth around the man's, maintaining a seal and giving a long breath, once, twice.

A second later she heard it. Not the wail of the siren

she was waiting for. No—something more familiar. The hum of an engine. An engine she would recognise anywhere.

There was a flash of red and silver beside her and she watched from the corner of her eye as the leather-clad figure dismounted from her bike. Seconds later, a helmet was tossed on the grass next to her and Carter was kneeling at her side. He nudged her aside. 'Let me,' he said, automatically placing his hands over hers and taking over the cardiac massage.

Lily heaved a sigh of relief and moved further up, next to the head of the man.

'What the hell happened?'

Lily shrugged. 'I just heard the crash a few minutes ago and came straight out. I've phoned for an ambulance, but there was no one around to help.'

He paused, a dark shadow passing over his face, while Lily did the mouth-to-mouth. 'This is Jack Marley— Donovan's grandfather. I can't let anything happen to him.' It was an emotional response, instead of the hard-nosed clinical reaction she was used to from medics.

Lily winced. She knew realistically that without the proper equipment there was only so much they could do. In the distance she heard the wail of a siren. 'I think we've got some help coming.'

They carried on for the next few minutes, Carter continuing with the chest compressions and Lily with the artificial respirations, until the ambulance pulled up and the paramedics grabbed their equipment and came to take over.

He gave them a quick nod. 'John Carter, San Francisco General.' In a situation like this, the paramedics were automatically in charge, but there was no rule to say that Carter couldn't assist. The paramedic nodded in recognition. It was apparent that Carter had no intention of standing back and watching, but the transition was seamless. Lily stood back as Carter helped them attach the monitor and insert a cannula to gain venous access.

'Come on, Jack,' she heard him murmur, as the monitor sprang to life, showing a bright green squiggly line.

'VF,' said one of the paramedics, checking the automatic defibrillator. 'Stand clear.'

Lily took a sharp breath. Ventricular fibrillation, meaning the heart wasn't pumping blood around the body, commonly caused by a myocardial infarction. In some cases, early defibrillation could reverse the condition. She glanced at her watch. Had it really only been five minutes since she'd found him?

Jack Marley's body jerked as the shock was delivered. Carter moved around and tipped his head back, taking a laryngoscope from the paramedic, sliding an ET tube into place and attaching the bag. 'Anything?'

The EMT shook his head, then took up position again, going through another five cycles of cardiac compressions and hyperventilation, while the paramedic administered some IV epinephrine. 'Check the rhythm again,' he said, stopping compressions for a second to allow the monitor to pick up the electrical activity of the heart. 'Still VF. Stand clear—shocking again.'

Jack Marley's body arched, then collapsed onto the ground again. Lily felt herself holding her breath, waiting for the signal to reappear on the monitor. And then it did. Slowly.

She felt herself jump as it appeared. Only a small percentage of patients survived a cardiac arrest out of hospital. Was Jack Marley going to be one of the lucky ones?

'We've got a rhythm—sinus brady. Thirty-three. Let's give him some more epinephrine and get going.'

The drug was administered and seconds later the heart rate started to rise. Forty, fifty, fifty-five.

The EMT pulled the portable stretcher from the back of the ambulance and they locked and loaded him. Carter touched Lily's arm. 'I'm sorry, I need to go with them. Jack Marley is a friend.'

Lily nodded automatically. Carter scribbled something on a bit of paper and handed it to her. 'Jack normally picks Donovan up from school. Can you give them a call and arrange something with them?'

Lily tried to make sense of what was going on. Carter was already stepping into the back of the ambulance, in mid-conversation with the paramedic.

'Isn't there a Mrs Marley?' she shouted after him. She knew only snippets of information about Carter's neighbours.

He shook his head. 'She died a few years ago, and Jack Marley's son works out of the city—he won't be back until late. I don't have any contact details for him.' The EMT slammed the doors shut and ran around to the front of the ambulance, turning the siren back on and taking off, leaving Lily standing bewildered on the road.

She stared at the surrounding chaos—her crutches lying on the grass, her motorbike abandoned in the middle of the street, and the bent streetlight and crumpled car with a small trickle of steam still venting from the hood.

This was going to be a long day. So much for surprises.

Lily lay on the leather sofa, Donovan curled in her lap, both of them wrapped in a rug. It wasn't cold but the situation called for comfort, and if that involved a furry blanket on a warm evening, so be it.

She looked at the clock again. After ten p.m. Carter

had texted her earlier to say he'd got hold of Jack's son and was staying at the hospital with him. Jack Marley had had a significant MI. It was still touch and go.

Donovan was half-asleep. She'd phoned the school and picked him up in a taxi, bringing him back to Carter's house. And if the private school's principal had been shocked to see a strange woman with a purple leg cast picking up one of her pupils you would never have known it. She'd been the ultimate professional and had taken the time check her credentials and to break the news to Donovan herself before Lily had appeared.

'Is Grandpa going to go up to heaven, like Grandma?'

Lily started. She looked down. Donovan's eyes were heavy, as if he were in that little period between waking and sleeping. She stroked his dark hair, thinking frantically of what to say. She didn't have much experience with children. Certainly not in this kind of capacity. And she didn't want to upset him.

'I certainly hope not. He's at the hospital with your dad and Carter. You know Carter will look after him as best he can.'

'But Carter's a bone doctor—not a heart doctor. You said it was Grandpa's heart that was hurt.'

'It is. But there are lots of different kinds of doctors at the hospital. The right one will be looking after your grandpa.'

Donovan nodded in sleepy assent, before laying his head back on Lily's shoulder and closing his eyes. Lily sent a silent prayer of thanks upwards that the tow truck had managed to come and tow his grandpa's car away before she'd brought him home from school. A smashed car was the last thing a little boy needed to see.

Her hand kept automatically stroking his hair and back. It was soothing. It was nice. She could feel his little chest rise and fall next to hers. He looked so much younger while he slept. Just like the little kid he actually was, rather than the mini grown-up that hung out at Carter's house.

Her mind started to wander, her imagination starting to run riot. Carter had a fabulous house. A house that should probably be filled with children. She closed her eyes shut.

In her head she could see them. Three bright and sunny kids, wreaking havoc around the house. Jumping on top of their father, wrestling him to the ground, swimming in the outdoor pool and playing catch in the back yard. The all-American family. But where was the mom? Where was the happy housewife baking cookies in the kitchen?

A shiver ran down her spine. Even in her daydreams something wasn't quite right. She couldn't imagine herself like a traditional mother.

Tears prickled in her eyes. She'd always wanted a family. And sitting here, like this, with Donovan felt so right. She could do this. She could have a child and devote herself to him. But it would have to be her child. Not someone else's.

The tears started to spill down her cheeks. How could she explain that to him? She couldn't even make sense of it herself. Carter wanted to fight for his baby. He wanted to be the father he'd always dreamed of being. And she should help him. She wanted to help him.

But her stomach was churning. She looked at the little boy lying in her arms. A pale-faced little angel. Imagine he was hers—and someone wanted to take him away? Even the thought of it made her feel sick.

And she knew this was how Carter must feel. But what about Olivia Simpson? What about the woman, who was probably lying in her bed tonight, hands on her baby bump, wondering if someone would try and take away her baby?

Why was it she could easily relate to how the woman must feel but not the man?

Was there something wrong with her?

A prickling feeling of dread crept up her spine. Was this jealousy? Was that what was wrong with her?

Was she really so shallow that a little more than two weeks after meeting someone she didn't want to share him? She didn't want anyone else to have his child?

Was this fear? Fear that there was distinct possibility she couldn't give him a child? Irrational fear that another woman was giving him a gift that should be hers? This was her egg. In effect, this was their baby. But it just didn't feel like that because none of the emotional attachment was there. She hadn't even known Carter when her egg and his sperm had been joined to create the embryo. And some other woman was currently growing and nurturing their child. And it pained her.

It pained her because, deep down, she was still worried that she might never have that experience. It didn't matter that no one had expressed concerns regarding her fertility. Because she had concerns. She had tiny seeds of doubt hidden in the deep recesses of her mind, seeds that seem to have taken deep root and started to sprout bright green shoots.

She didn't want to think these thoughts because if she kept them inside she could pretend they didn't exist. She could pretend they didn't matter.

Carter had no idea about her sister and the early menopause. He still had no idea about her storing eggs for future use.

She tried to breathe deeply. He was a kind and good

man. If she told him her fears, what would he say? Would he take a deep breath and tell her it would be all right? That they could do it all again?

After his current experience he would have to be mad. And deep down she knew it. So an irrational envy of this other woman was sweeping through her.

This baby could be Carter's only chance at having a biological child.

She squeezed her eyes closed, stopping the tears from flowing. It couldn't be that. She wasn't like that. She'd never been like that before.

But her attraction to Carter was growing every day, every hour, every minute. As much as she tried to deny it, she'd never felt like this before. Sure, she'd had fun and friendships and passing attractions before, but she'd never felt anything like this. She'd never felt a connection like the one she had with Carter. Never felt that bone-deep ache to see someone again only a few minutes after they'd left. Never felt as if she could sing out loud when they ran a finger along your skin. Never felt as if she could die without their touch.

This was it.

There was no getting away from it.

This was love.

So why wasn't she shouting it from the rooftops?

Why did it feel as if it was breaking her heart?

Carter turned the key in the lock as silently as he could. He pushed the door open and tiptoed inside, gesturing to the man behind him to follow.

Lily was asleep on the sofa, Donovan in her arms, the two of them wrapped in a blanket.

The sight of them took his breath away. All day long he'd tried not to think about things. His head had been so busy with MIs and cardiac investigations, getting hold of Donovan's dad and staying with Jack, that he'd almost managed to avoid thinking about it. But hospital waiting rooms had minds of their own.

They were designed to eat into your soul.

To be mindless and blank, with five-year-old magazines, out-of-order coffee machines and uncomfortable chairs, so there was no room for distraction. The only thing left to do was think.

And now here it was, the picture that had been dancing around in his head all day. The ideal family picture of a mother and child. And right now it was searing the image permanently on his brain.

It didn't matter that Donovan wasn't his child and Lily wasn't the mother. It was the idea. It was the mere principle of the thing taking shape right before his eyes.

But his future wasn't going to look like this. His future might include a beautiful baby, but he would be on his own—there wouldn't be a mother in the picture.

What happened if he had another day like today? Where things blew up out of nothing and he had to be away for twelve hours at a time? Who would take care of his baby? Who would cuddle up with his child and nurse it to sleep?

Once again the little trickle of dread was seeping through his bones. Could he really do this on his own? Could he really be everything that his baby would need?

But there was something else bothering him. That sight of Lily holding Donovan in her arms. The look of contentment on both their faces.

It troubled him more than he'd ever thought possible. What about that relationship between a mother and her child? For the last few weeks he'd only thought about his relationship with the baby—not anyone else's. He hadn't wanted to consider anyone else.

But what if he took that possibility away from his child? Lily might not see herself as the mother of his child—but Olivia Simpson did. He could feel the hairs on the back of his neck stand on end. He'd always enjoyed a close relationship with his mother, right up until a few years ago when she'd died. He couldn't imagine not having that closeness. More than that, how would he feel if someone had taken that opportunity away from him? It was more than he could bear to think about.

He moved quickly, crossing the room, lifting Donovan from Lily's arms and handing him to his father.

'Here you go, David. If you need any help, just give me a call. Lily and I are happy to give you a hand.' He pressed his hand on the pale man's shoulder. 'Things are looking good. Your dad's stable now. Hopefully he'll have a quiet night and we'll see him again in the morning.'

David nodded and headed back to the door, carrying the sleeping child. 'Thanks, Carter. And thank Lily for me. I'll call you in the morning.'

Carter nodded and closed the door quietly behind him.

Lily started as she heard the final click of the lock, her eyes flew open and immediately fixed on her empty arms. 'Where's Donovan?' She looked instantly awash with panic.

Carter sat down beside her and wrapped his arm around her shoulders. 'Shh,' he said. 'You were sleeping. Donovan's fine. I've just given him back to his dad, who's taken him home. You'll probably see him again tomorrow.'

'How's Jack? Has something happened? Is he still alive?'

Carter nodded. 'He was so lucky, Lily. If you hadn't been here, I dread to think what would have happened.' His hand started stroking her hair. 'There's not many people have a massive MI at the wheel of a car and live to tell the tale.'

She rested her head on his shoulder, taking comfort from his movements. 'It's been a long time since I've had to be a first responder. My mind went blank for a second.'

'Well, you looked as if you were doing fine when I saw you.' He dropped a kiss on her forehead. She smiled. There it was again, that delicious zing between them that appeared whenever he touched her. She snuggled closer and laid her hand on his chest. 'Thank goodness you arrived. My arms were burning. I don't know how much longer I could have carried on on my own.' She shifted position, sitting up to look at him. It had been hours since she'd seen his face properly. And for some reason she felt the need to drink it in. To sweep her gaze over every dark hair on his head, the shadow of stubble on his jaw, his blue eyes and thick brown eyelashes. She'd missed him.

She wrinkled her nose. 'I'm sure that dispatcher was making it up when she said the ambulance would be there in five minutes. It was much longer than five minutes.'

He stroked his finger along her jaw, before kissing her on the nose. 'It doesn't matter how long it was— you did fine.'

'I take it my bike was your surprise?'

Carter sat bolt upright. 'Your bike! Oh, no! I forgot all about it. Is it still out on the street? I was so tired I never even noticed.'

She laughed. 'Calm down. A few neighbours appeared after the ambulance left—they'd heard the siren. One of them wheeled my bike into your garage. It's locked up safe and sound, right next to yours.'

'Phew!' He collapsed back again. 'I'd totally forgotten all about it. I'd collected the bike from the hangar at the airfield as a surprise for you.' He looked at her with rueful eyes. 'Guess this day didn't turn out as I planned—in more ways than one.'

She saw a dark cloud pass over his face and was instantly on edge. 'Why? What else has happened today?'

Carter sighed. He really didn't want to get into this now. It was too late and he was exhausted. But Lily had that look on her face. The one she got when she wasn't going to let a thing drop. He took a deep breath. 'Cole.'

'Cole? Your attorney? What's wrong?'

Carter glanced at his watch. He'd do anything to avoid this. 'It's too late for this now. Let's go to bed. We can talk in the morning.' He stood up and held his hand out to Lily.

But she was frozen, a leaden feeling in her stomach. 'No, Carter. Let's talk now. Tell me what's wrong. What did Cole want? Is there a problem with the baby?'

Cole shook his head. 'I'm still getting updates on the baby. It's the case. Cole's beginning to take some angles that I don't like.'

He sat back down next to Lily. She looked tired. This really wasn't the best time to be thinking about this. But Cole had phoned him five times today, each time with another query about making their case stronger. And three of those queries had been about Lily.

Carter rested his head back against the soft leather of the sofa. He couldn't even think straight right now. Olivia Simpson was thirty-two weeks pregnant and, due to complications, the baby was likely to be delivered early. His son or daughter would arrive in roughly two weeks due to the medical issues. He looked around his house.

He hadn't even started preparing. He hadn't even started to plan to bring this baby home. Why not? By this stage most people would have decorated their nursery and filled it with furniture. The stroller and car seat would have been ordered. And the cupboards would be stocked with clothes. He might only have found out a few weeks ago but why hadn't he done any of that?

Lily brushed his arm. 'Carter, are you okay? You look a million miles away. Tell me about Cole.'

He took a deep breath. 'He's worried about how the publicity is going to affect my case.'

'You mean me?' She pointed to herself. 'Is this about that photo of me?'

Carter bit his lip. How could he put this without offending her? The last thing he wanted to do right now— at the end of a very long day—was offend the woman he wanted to hold in his arms. 'Yes, and no. He needs to talk to you. He needs to brief you on what might happen in the courtroom. He wants to prepare you for any questions you might get asked.'

Lily sat forward. He could tell she was feeling defensive. It wasn't what he was saying—it was what he wasn't saying. And she'd picked up on it straight away.

'What kind of questions? Questions about me—my background?' She shook her head. 'I don't have any dirty secrets, Carter. I don't have a criminal background or secret love children stashed somewhere. The only thing of note that I've ever done is donate eggs.' She glared at him fiercely. 'And no matter what our previous conversations—what you might think—I think that's a good thing, not something to be cross-examined about in court.'

Her face was flushed with pink and he could see the little sparks of fire in her eyes.

He couldn't think about this. He couldn't deal with the whirlpool of doubts currently circulating in his head and how this might have an impact on them. More than anything he couldn't deal with the sensations that had swept him in the last few minutes, when he'd seen Lily with Donovan. Try as he might, this woman was starting to take over his every thought.

'I agree,' he whispered as he leaned forward until his nose was exactly opposite hers, pausing to look into her eyes for just a second then taking her lips with his.

It had the desired effect. It silenced her immediately. He wrapped his arms around her slim waist and pulled her closer. There. That was just what he needed. Her warm body next to his.

This felt right. This felt exactly the way it should be. This was what he wanted to concentrate on. He didn't have the mental energy to deal with anything else.

She pulled back, breathless from his kiss. 'I think you're trying to distract me.' Her eyes were heavy with desire and a small smile had appeared on her lips. Along with something else. What was that? Relief?

'I think you could be right,' he agreed as he took her lips with his again. He nuzzled closer to her neck. 'Why don't you give me instructions on how exactly you would like to be distracted…?'

CHAPTER EIGHT

LILY shifted uncomfortably in the big, high-backed chair. Its comfort wasn't in question. The chair probably had a vast amount of research-based evidence to attest to its ergonomics—and to justify its exorbitant price tag. The chair was fine. It was her. She hated this place.

From the second she'd entered the wide, glass-fronted office with its ultra-glamorous receptionist, dressed from head to toe in Chanel, she'd felt out of place. Being on crutches, with a long flowing Indian print skirt and one sequinned flip-flop probably didn't help. Being left sitting twenty minutes after her scheduled appointment time certainly didn't.

Her heart was fluttering in her chest—and not in a good way. Her palms were sweating and her skin prickling. Lily was nervous. And she wasn't used to being nervous. It was a sensation she'd no intention of getting accustomed to.

Everything was annoying her. The polish on the toenails sticking out from her cast was chipped. And she hadn't even noticed until she'd sat down in the pristine surroundings. Bright pink nails with ugly chips.

Her leg was itchy. It had been just over three weeks since her cast had been put on and the hairs on her leg must be growing like wildfire under there. Right now she wanted to do all the things that the hospital staff told you not to. They even gave patients a printed information sheet to reinforce the points. But if Lily could get her hands on a knitting needle then all hell would break loose.

Two more days until her cast was changed. Luckily, her fracture had healed ahead of schedule and she could be transferred into a walking cast. She was absolutely determined she was taking her razor and shaving cream to the hospital with her. There was no way she could carry on like this.

She eyed Miss Perfect's desk. There. A thirty-centimetre ruler. That would be perfect. Surely she could shove that down her cast without causing any damage?

Miss Perfect had disappeared. Lily flicked her head, scanning up and down the never-ending corridor. No one in sight.

She grabbed the ruler, lifted the hem of her skirt and pushed the ruler inside her cast, rubbing furiously. She gave a huge sigh of relief. Bliss.

Carter would kill her if he could see her now. He'd spent two days telling her horror stories of patients who'd pushed things down their casts. All in an attempt to stop her from scratching the permanent itch. It was a well-known fact that nurses made the worst patients. He should have known better.

Her phone started to vibrate in her bag sitting on the floor. Message from the dark side. The voice of Yoda from Star Wars floated around her. It was Carter. He'd changed the message tone on her phone the other night to announce his texts. His sense of humour left a lot to be desired.

Someone cleared their throat loudly next to her, causing her to jump out of her skin. 'Ms Grayson, would you like to come this way, please?'

A thin-faced man in a dark suit stood next to her. He looked distinctly unimpressed. Lily felt the colour flood into her face as she pulled the ruler from her cast. 'Uh…. here.' She handed him the ruler, much to his disgust. He dangled it between two fingers before placing it on the edge of Miss Perfect's desk.

He waited until she had slid her arms into her crutches and looped her bag over her wrist before ushering her down the corridor—the long, long corridor—and into a huge luxurious office.

She flopped down into the wide leather chair he gestured towards and waited until he took his seat at the other side of the desk.

He shuffled papers. And shuffled papers again. Then he composed himself and met her impatient gaze. 'Ms Grayson, there are a number of things we need to discuss.'

Lily felt a wave of irritation wash over her. 'Why don't you start by introducing yourself then?' she snapped.

He drew back with the look of a startled rabbit. 'O-of course,' he stammered, before standing and leaning over the desk, extending his hand towards her. 'Sorry about that. I'm Cole Turner, John Carter's attorney.'

She shook his hand. His grip was firmer than she'd expected.

He sat back down in his chair, his gaze steady on Lily's face. As if he was getting the measure of her. His expression changed, almost as if he'd decided to take a different approach with her, and a smile appeared on his face. 'Ms Grayson, you're here today so I can establish the best role for you to play in Dr Carter's custody case.'

That instantly annoyed her. She was to play a 'role'—being herself was obviously not good enough.

He cleared his throat. 'I'm trying to build the best possible case for my client to ensure that he wins custody of his child. Time is of the essence here, as we don't know yet when the child will be born, but we have to be ready to move at a moment's notice. It's my belief—as paternity has already been established—that John Carter will have a strong case to gain custody.'

'I wanted to ask you about that.' Lily's voice cut through his. He had obviously regained his footing and was about to talk for hours. Lily hated that. She hated wasting time. She liked things short and sharp and to the point.

'You told Carter that in cases like these, around seventy per cent of the time the genetic parents gain custody.'

He nodded and started to speak again, 'Yes, that's right—'

She cut him off again. 'Well, I've been doing some research of my own. I think you're wrong.'

'Wrong?' The pitch of his voice rose, almost as if in indignation at her suggestion.

'Yes. From what I can see on the internet, it looks much more like a fifty-fifty split.'

He gave her The Look. The Look that people gave you when they doubted your intelligence and were about to say something really condescending. 'The internet should be used with caution, Ms Grayson. You really don't know what you're looking at.'

She raised her eyebrows at him. Did he realise just how much he was annoying her? There. He did it again, obviously unconsciously. His eyes swept over her, leaving a look of distaste on his face. She could almost see him measuring her up for a suitable suit for her court appearance. How would a purple cast fit into that?

'I think you're leaving John unprepared. I think you need to speak to him about the possibility of him not gaining custody of his child.'

'Let me deal with the court case, Ms Grayson. I'm the expert in these matters—not you.' He leaned towards her. 'Let's talk about what you can do to help John.'

She bristled at his words. She was obviously irritating him as much as he was her. But it was just the way he said that word. Almost as if he knew what was going on behind closed doors at Carter's house.

The irony was ridiculous. She'd been pictured half-dressed on Carter's doorstep. Half the world knew what was going on behind closed doors. Why did it matter what this attorney thought?

'Miss Grayson?' He'd fixed her with that steely glare again, catching her daydreaming.

'Yes.'

'It's important I brief you on what I want you to say in court.' He picked up a file and Lily baulked when she realised her name was on it. 'It's vital that the issue of monetary gain for your egg donation isn't a factor in this court case. We'll have to find an alternative reason for you donating eggs.' He lifted his fingers creating quotation marks in the air.

How dare he? How dare he find an 'alternative' reason for her to donate eggs? This was what she didn't want. Some parts of her life were private, not for public consumption. Her reason for egg donation was nobody's business but hers.

She hated the way he was looking at her. She hated the fact it seemed as if he was judging her.

'We will have to discuss your appearance…' his eyes

swept over her again '...and discourage some of your usual pastimes.'

Lily let that fly over her head. The man was clearly crazy and knew little, or nothing, about her. She'd just noticed a file with Olivia's name on it. She felt as if she could be sick. She remembered Carter's words from last week that he didn't like the direction Cole was taking.

'What are you going to do about Olivia?' The question came out of nowhere. He looked surprised.

Lily kept on. 'She's a widow. She's a doctor. She'll make a fabulous mother. What are you going to say in court about her?' Lily could feel the wave of fear creeping over her. This was a court case. He was an attorney. He had a job to do.

In a moment of clarity it hit her and for the first time she realised part of that job might be destroying Olivia. She felt sick. She'd fought with Carter a few days ago saying she didn't want her life splashed all over the court. What about Olivia?

Cole's jaw was set. He knew exactly what she was asking. 'I'll do whatever is necessary to win John Carter custody of his child. That's my job.'

Lily sat back in the chair.

'And I thought you would also have John's best interests at heart.'

There it was. The emphasis that he knew about their relationship. The unspoken assumption that she would do whatever it took.

Her stomach churned. And almost in unison her phone sounded again. Message from the dark side.

She couldn't stay here. She couldn't be in this room a second longer. No matter how she felt about Carter she wasn't sure she could be part of this.

Lily stood up and grabbed her crutches. 'I'm sorry, Mr Turner. I'm not feeling too well. I'm going to have to go.'

She limped towards the door, then turned and faced him again. 'But let me assure you, Mr Turner, no matter what happens, I absolutely have John Carter's best interests at heart.'

Carter stared at the text message. Come home.

Something was wrong. No L. No kiss. He tried to phone her—no reply. Seconds later his phone beeped again—a message from his attorney. He didn't even have to listen to it, he could already sense the meeting hadn't gone well.

He hung his coat up behind the door in his office and changed into his leathers. Twenty minutes later, after darting through the San Francisco traffic, he pulled into his drive.

Lily was sitting in the back yard next to the pool, her knees drawn up under her chin. Her eyes were wet and red rimmed, a piece of paper dangling in her hand and her mobile phone sitting next to her.

He walked across the grass towards her, enveloping her in a hug. 'Want to tell me what's wrong?'

Her chin was quivering and her hands were trembling. This was the woman who jumped out of aeroplanes and off cliffs. This was the woman they called Dynamo. What on earth was wrong with her?

'Lily?'

'I don't know what's wrong, Carter. Nothing feels right.'

He knelt down beside her and ran his finger along her cheek, giving her a half-smile. 'Nothing?'

She squeezed her eyes shut. 'That's part of it.' She grabbed hold of his hand and held it tightly. 'I want to enjoy this. I want to feel free to see where this takes us.' She clutched his hand close to her chest. 'But everything else is getting in the way.'

'Did Cole upset you? What did he say?'

Her eyes brimmed with tears again and her voice was tight and strained. 'It's what he didn't say—and it's what he intends to do.'

Carter unzipped his leather jacket and slid his arms out of it. This was going to take a while, and on a cool summer evening like this, it was better to be comfortable. He wrapped his arm around Lily, letting her rest her head on his shoulder while the two of them stared out over the back yard and beyond towards the wooded slopes of Hillsborough. He'd already had concerns about some of the hints Cole had dropped regarding the case. It appeared his fears weren't unfounded.

'Tell me.'

He heard Lily take a deep breath. 'When I went into his office he had files with my name and Olivia's name. Things just started to click into place for me. He wanted to be sure about what I'd say. He mentioned the fact I'd been paid for the egg donation and wanted to try and brush that under the carpet—create another reason for me donating eggs. He made me feel as if my life would be put under the microscope. Then I realised that if their attorney might look into my background, Cole has probably been looking into Olivia's.'

She turned to face him, her eyes fraught with emotion. 'Carter—look at me. Even thinking about all this makes me a mess. I'm never like this. I never let things affect me like this. And if this is me—with only myself to worry about—how is she? How is Olivia Simpson doing?'

Carter felt himself draw backwards.

'What's Cole going to say to her in court, Carter?

We've seen the papers. She's a good person—we know she's a good person. One who's been through enough already. What's he going to find? Because we both know he's going to massacre her. Why would you let that happen? Look at what this is doing to me. What's this doing to her? And what's this doing to *your* baby?'

The words hung in the air.

Carter's mind flooded with images of a stressed Olivia Simpson. The last thing he wanted to think about. But everything Lily was saying was true. Cole skirted around the edges of all these things.

He was only doing his job and trying to build the best possible case for him. But Lily was obviously uncomfortable with his methods and, truth be told, so was he. His eyes fixed on the piece of paper dangling from her fingers, numbers scrawled across it.

He felt his chest constrict when he recognised the number instantly. 'Why have you got the number for the clinic, Lily?'

She turned her head away from him, crumpling the piece of paper in her hand.

'Lily?'

Her voice was trembling. 'I need to speak to them. I need to speak to them about my eggs.'

Carter was confused. 'What are you talking about? You know what happened to your eggs.'

Her voice was quiet, almost a whisper. 'No. No, I don't.'

Something wasn't right. He felt as if there was a whole conversation going on here that he knew nothing about.

'What are you talking about?' He put his hands on her shoulders and pulled her around towards him. Her face was pale, with worry lines across her forehead. She buried her head in her hands.

He stayed exactly where he was. Waiting. He had to give her time. He could hear her taking some deep breaths. After a few minutes she lifted her head.

'I have some extra eggs stored at the clinic, Carter. When I donated eggs, I stored some for myself.'

'But why on earth would you want to do that?' He felt confused. Why would a healthy woman want to store eggs?

'I did it as a precaution.'

'A precaution for what? Were you planning to wait until you were fifty before you had kids of your own?' Carter couldn't imagine any other reason for her wanting to store eggs, but even this one seemed bizarre.

'I did it because of my sister.'

'Your sister?' Now he was really confused. Lily had mentioned her sister a few times in passing but never in any detail.

She bit her bottom lip. 'My sister had some fertility problems. She suffered from an early menopause. It meant she couldn't have any children of her own. And when she tried to find an egg donor, she found it very difficult.'

'So you donated eggs for her to use?' He still found this strange. Surely there were plenty of egg donors available.

'No.' Lily shook her head. 'My sister is fifteen years older than me. I was a late baby. Fifteen years ago it was much more difficult to find egg donors. And it really affected her mental health. She was very depressed—for a long time. That's why I decided to be an egg donor. At the time I was too young to help my sister, but once I was old enough I knew that I wanted to do it. No one should go through what my sister did.'

Carter shifted his gaze away from her and stared out

over the hills. He looked deep in thought, as if pieces of the jigsaw puzzle were finally starting to fall into place. 'So it wasn't just about the money, was it?'

She shook her head. 'The money was an added bonus. That was all.'

'But why store eggs for yourself?'

'Because I was scared.'

He shook his head. 'But, Lily, what did you have to be scared about?'

Tears filled her eyes again. 'What if the same thing happens to me? What if I have an early menopause like my sister? Donating eggs was like a lifeline for me. I got to have a safety net. I got to store some eggs for myself. Fertility is a thing that so many people take for granted.' He could see the hurt and worry in her eyes. She pointed at her chest. 'I want to have children, Carter. I want to have a family. But what if my body takes away that chance? The clinic tested me and they couldn't find any problems but there are no guarantees in this life. I wanted to be safe. I wanted to be sure.' She squeezed her eyes tightly shut. 'My sister was so sick. She was suicidal. It took her a long time to get over it. I don't ever want to be like that.'

And he could see it. The face she put on to the world. The bravado. The confidence. What was her nickname? Dynamo? Because that's the way she acted. Because that's the way she wanted the world to see her. When underneath it all she was frightened. Frightened she wouldn't get the happy family that nobody knew she craved. Frightened she wouldn't have the mental strength to fight her way through any problems.

His heart twisted inside his chest. He wanted to put his arms around her. He wanted to tell her everything would be okay. That she had no reason to worry.

But he couldn't. Because he was annoyed. And there was a burning feeling right in the pit of his stomach. Something so important, as fundamental as this and she hadn't shared it with him. But more than that, his brain had immediately switched into self-protection mode. It was currently screaming, Get away! You can't do all this again!

'So, tell me again, why are you phoning the clinic?' His voice sounded clipped and he knew it.

'Because what if they've made the same mistakes with my eggs as they did with your embryo? What if they've been mislabelled—or lost? What if some lab technician has taken away my safety net, my chance to have a baby?' He could hear the desperation in her tone, but he couldn't acknowledge it. 'I need to know. I want to see proof. I don't trust them any more.'

She sounded exhausted. As if she'd spent all day with this pent-up emotion and fury circulating about her system. And the natural release was to tell him.

But he couldn't get over the fact they'd practically spent the last month together and she hadn't told him any of this. Not in the long, hot nights spent wrapped in each other's arms or in those quiet times—the long leisurely lunches or days together.

He hated lies. He hated deceit. And even if she hadn't actually told him a lie, it felt like it. She'd missed out a part of her life that was so important to her—something that affected her deep down inside, and she hadn't shared it with him.

But there was something else. Something twisting away at his gut. He didn't even want to acknowledge it. He didn't even want to think about it. It was dancing around his head like a ping-pong ball being batted back and forth across a table.

What if Lily did have fertility problems? What if she was right to store her eggs? Did he want to consider a future filled with clinic visits again? He'd already been through all that with Tabitha, and their marriage hadn't stood the strain. He knew firsthand the stress of a relationship with fertility problems. If his feelings for Lily progressed the way he wanted them to, could their relationship stand the strain?

He was angry with himself. This whole situation was turning him into a person he didn't want to be. Nobody—man or woman—came with a fully stamped fertility certificate. How dared he even have these thoughts?

What if it were him? What if he'd had some past infection or disease that could have affected his fertility? What if Lily were standing here now, contemplating whether he was worth having a relationship with, based on his potential fertility?

He would be sickened. And he would walk away in a heartbeat.

So why was he now looking at Lily differently? Why, when he could see the hurt and pain in her eyes, wasn't he just gathering her up in his arms and telling her that everything would be fine? It didn't matter. Even if her eggs were lost, or destroyed, nothing would change between them. He would be there for her.

Why wasn't he doing that?

Because he couldn't. Because right now his arms felt like leaden pipes, hanging at his sides. Too heavy to lift or move. Right now he hated himself. Hated himself for feeling like this. Hated the fact his brain was even suggesting he use the excuse of 'the lie' to walk away from all this.

The sun was going down, causing beautiful warm streams of red, gold and orange to scatter across the sky. Lily was standing in front of it, captured in its light like a sunbeam. Like a movie star captured in a million-dollar photo shoot.

But the heat and warmth was lost on him.

He could see her face, frantically searching his. Trying to capture his eyes. The gaze he was keeping firmly fixed on the trees in the distance. He needed time. He needed space. He needed to digest everything that had happened.

'Carter?' Her voice was starting to crack. 'Say something, please.'

'What do you want me to say, Lily?' His voice was a monotone. No matter what the confusion was in his brain right now, he knew better than to formulate it into words. He could easily say something he would live to regret.

'Something. Anything. Tell me what you're thinking.' She stood in front of him, blocking out the setting sun's rays.

'Are you going to help me win my baby?' In an instant, everything in Carter's head had become black and white again. Like it had been right at the beginning, when he'd first heard the news about his baby— before he'd met Lily. These past four weeks had made everything turn to shades of grey. He'd been having doubts, questioning himself if he was doing the right thing. Allowing Lily and his feelings for her to influence how he felt.

He felt as if he'd pulled off the rose-coloured glasses. He had to focus. Lily had a purpose. To help him gain custody of his child. Nothing more, nothing less.

If she wasn't going to help him, should she even be here? Should he even be spending time with her?

Lily stammered. She looked desperate, as if she

wanted to say the words he needed to hear, but was struggling. 'I—I'm not sure…I n-need to think about things.'

He grabbed her hand and unfolded her clenched fingers, releasing the crumpled paper in her grasp. 'And will this help you make up your mind?'

She looked confused and hurt. 'Wh-what?'

'This?' He thrust the bit of paper at her again. 'Will determining your fertility help you make your mind up about my baby?'

He knew it was crazy. He knew it was an unreasonable and irrational question, but right now he didn't care. He wanted an answer. He wanted to be able to make a plan.

She hesitated, confusion spreading across her face and into her eyes. 'I just need to sort things out in my head. I can't think straight about anything right now.'

He watched her. He could see the panic and stress in her face and body. Her arms and shoulders were tense, the muscles at the side of her neck rigid. Why was he doing this to her? Why was he doing this to Lily—the woman he loved?

The thought was like a bolt from the blue. Like the symbolic setting sun sending multicoloured streamers across the sky. He dropped his hand, releasing the paper and letting it flutter away in the evening breeze. And they both watched as it undulated in the warm air currents, up and down across the wide back yard and over into the Hillsborough woods that skirted the back of his property.

He picked up her phone, which was lying on the grass. And dialled the number that was engrained in his brain. It might be late but the clinic was always staffed, particularly in the light of recent events. The call was answered quickly. 'I need to make an appointment for my friend, Lily Grayson, to see Rhonda Fulton.' He waited while he heard the shuffle of some papers. 'Thursday's fine. Three o'clock? That will be perfect.' He hung up the phone and stared towards his pool. 'Then let's find out.' His voice was low, almost a whisper.

'Carter?'

'Yeah?' He couldn't bring his eyes to meet hers. He couldn't get over the wave of emotions that had just crashed through him. It was if someone had just switched the light on in his brain.

She'd been in his thoughts constantly for the last three weeks. He'd craved her company, wanting to speak to her all the time. Even in this maelstrom of events, his thoughts had always come back to her.

Everything about this was wrong. The timing was awful. He had to focus on his child, not on some wild, passionate fling that would probably amount to nothing. Especially with the possibility of fertility problems hanging over them like a dark cloud.

He tried to remember Tabitha. Everything was always wonderful when you first met someone. But it always faded, it always passed when the cold, harsh realities of life came crashing down.

But even then, even with the woman he had married, he hadn't felt like this. He hadn't felt so involved, so connected as he did with Lily. How awful was that?

'What happens now?' Her voice had changed. It was more steely, more determined. This was the Lily he knew. The woman who had her own mind and wouldn't change it for anyone.

She didn't even need to explain any further. They both knew that something had happened, something had changed between them. She spoke calmly, rationally. 'My cast is due to get changed the day after tomorrow.

All being well, I'll have a walking cast and I'll be able to manage on my own.'

The air seemed to close in around Carter, compressing his lungs. Once Lily had her walking cast on she would be more mobile, more able to manage on her own. She wouldn't need him any more. She wouldn't need to stay here any more. His time was up. And he hadn't managed to persuade her to help him.

He lifted his eyes to face her. She had one hand on her hip and a determined edge to her jaw. Whatever inner strength she'd been lacking earlier, she had now clearly found.

He hesitated. This could change everything. This could change his life. How could he bet on a woman who couldn't even agree to help him gain custody of his child? His head was telling him one thing but his heart another. He had to get through this. He had to find a way to make sense of this all. But one burning feeling in his chest was overtaking all the others. It wasn't rational. It didn't make sense at all—not in light of the current conversation. What he said now could determine his life for the next twenty years. But these were the only words that could come to his lips.

'I don't want you to go.' There. He'd said it.

She came up, her face just under his chin. Her green eyes were glinting in the rapidly fading light. 'Then you better give me a reason to stay.'

CHAPTER NINE

LILY walked up towards the entrance of the clinic. Finally free of her crutches, with her walking cast in place, she should be feeling relieved and thankful. Instead, her stomach was twisting in knots.

She breathed slowly. In and out. In and out. She needed to be calm. She needed to have a clear head. No matter how much this was all confusing her, she needed to be rational.

Rhonda Fulton was standing in the foyer, waiting for her. She seemed in a hurry to usher her along the corridor and into her office.

'Have a seat, please, Ms Grayson. How is your ankle?'

'It's better, thank you. Another three weeks and I hopefully I'll be back at work.'

'I'm sorry I never got a chance to speak to you when you phoned for the appointment. But I gather it was late in the evening when you called.'

She tilted her head to one side, as if asking a question. Lily steadfastly ignored the query. 'That's right.'

Rhonda positioned herself in the chair opposite, shuffling some papers on her desk and opening a red file in front of her. 'Let's start at the beginning. These are the papers you signed regarding your egg storage.'

Lily looked firmly at her. It was hard not to disguise

the aversion she had to this woman. Even though Rhonda
Fulton was only doing her job, right now everything
about her just annoyed Lily. So much for being a calm
and rational individual.

Lily pulled an almost identical folder from her bag.
'It's quite all right, Ms Fulton,' she said calmly, 'I have
my own copy of the paperwork.' She fixed her eyes on
Rhonda. 'But we both know it's not the paperwork I'm
here about.' Lily folded her hands in her lap, the temptation to start fidgeting and reveal her agitation very real.
'What I want to know is if my eggs have been correctly
labelled, correctly stored and will be available for future
use if I require them.' It was hard to keep the tremor out
of her voice.

Rhonda adjusted her glasses on the bridge of her nose.
'Our storage facilities are second to none. I understand
your concern because of recent events. But since then
our new director has had every sample currently stored
within our clinic checked and double-checked. Each
sample has been verified by two embryologists and our
clinical director.' She pulled a form from the coloured
folder, 'You currently have twenty eggs stored with us.
Each of them is labelled with your full name, date of
birth and social security number. We also allocate each
patient a colour.' Her eyes brushed over Lily. 'You were
allocated purple and your eggs are stored in Dewar tank
seventeen. There are no other patients' eggs in your storage tank with the same colour.'

'Can I see them?'

Rhonda Fulton took a deep breath and glanced at her
watch. 'We include laboratory microscopic photographs
in our files.' She handed Lily some photographs of her
labelled samples.

'Our laboratory and storage area are completely secure. As a nurse I'm sure you understand the theory behind contamination. We only allow our own personnel in these areas. The frozen eggs are stored in liquid nitrogen in the Dewar tank. The tanks are monitored twenty-four hours a day, seven days a week, three hundred and sixty-five days a year. Your eggs are safe, Ms Grayson.'

Lily pushed her shoulders back into the chair. She was hearing the words but finding it difficult to control her emotional response. She wanted to scream Show them to me! even though she knew it was impossible.

'Ms Grayson, I'm sure we explained to you at the time, but it's probably worth repeating that when the time comes that you want to use your eggs, not all will survive the thawing process. Cryopreservation is a very delicate technique. A woman's eggs can be quite fragile and may not tolerate the freezing process very well. Eggs have a high water content. Freezing this water can affect the eggs' outer coverings and lead to problems during thawing. On average around sixty per cent of eggs survive the thawing process.' It was almost as if she was rehearsing a carefully practised spiel. Then she paused, taking time to let Lily digest the information. 'As you probably know, most women tend to favour the option of freezing embryos instead of eggs—the success rates are generally higher. However, I should let you know that we have had success at this facility in achieving a successful pregnancy from a frozen egg, so it is possible.' Rhonda shot her a bright red-lipped smile. And for the first time she didn't look superior or condescending, she actually looked as if she was trying to offer some reassurance.

Lily nodded slowly. She'd heard all this before. She'd researched the facts before storing her eggs, and although she'd known that storing embryos was more likely to be successful, it hadn't seemed like an option at the time.

She didn't have a partner and hadn't wanted to use donor sperm.

The underlying thought had always been there at the back of her mind that someday she might meet someone—someone just like Carter—and she might want to have a family with him. The thought of using some anonymous donor's sperm to fertilise her eggs had never appealed to her, no matter what the success rate was.

So that was it. Her eggs were safe. Eggs that she might not ever even need to use. Or eggs that she might want the man she loved to impregnate—to create their happy family together. Something she'd never allowed to develop at the forefront of her mind.

Carter. There he was, in her mind again. Just when she thought she could block him out and focus on something else. Just when she thought she could stay rational and methodical about the information she was being given.

He was creeping in again. And she didn't know whether to be happy or sad. They'd spent the last few nights in each other's arms with a frenzy and passion that set her soul on fire.

But both of them knew the truth. They were avoiding the obvious conversation. The one that might end with someone saying something wrong. Something that couldn't be forgiven. Something that would make one, or the other, walk away.

It was easy to forget in Carter's arms. It was easy to spend the whole night pretending none of this was actually happening. And for a few seconds every morning waking up in his arms was great. Then reality hit. Leaving her wondering if this would be the last day. The last day of waking up wrapped around the man that she loved.

Every time the phone rang she jumped, worried it would be Cole with news about the court case or the baby. News that could change their world.

Lily stared down at her hands. Now she knew. Now she had no excuse. She'd told Carter once she'd been to the clinic she would be able to sort her head out and think straight. She'd be able to make a decision about what she was going to do.

But it had all been a delaying tactic. And she was sure he knew that. They'd already skirted around the edges of this conversation.

Of course she wanted to know if her eggs were safe. At the very least, she was paying every year for the privilege of storing her eggs here. The least they could do was verify that the storage was appropriate and secure.

But what now?

She felt a hand pressing on her shoulder. Rhonda gave her a smile. 'I'll just give you a few minutes, Ms Grayson. I'll go and get you some coffee. If you have any more questions, you can let me know.'

Lily was surprised. She must have drifted off into her daydream. Rhonda was obviously trying to give her a bit of space.

She stood up and stretched, walking over to the window, staring out towards San Francisco Bay. The clinic wasn't in a prime location. It had large premises, big enough for their consulting rooms, procedures and storage facilities and far enough away from the tourist areas to keep the privacy of the clients intact.

But as it was set into the side of a hill, like much of San Francisco, there was still a far-away view of the Bay, with its dark grey island of Alcatraz and contrasting red Golden Gate bridge. Lily fixed her eyes on those. This was home. After a few years at university in the east, San Francisco definitely felt like home.

Here she got to be who she wanted to be, with no restrictions, no guards. She got to pursue all her outdoor activities with no one questioning her. She got to put on her leathers and ride her beloved Ducati into the surrounding hills and Napa Valley area.

At twenty-seven she had her own apartment in the heart of San Francisco. Granted, it was three flights up and not the biggest apartment in the world, but it more than suited her needs. It was the perfect life.

So why, all of a sudden, did it feel not so perfect?

Why did her life feel empty?

Was it because of this? Was it the trouble at the clinic and her thoughts about her eggs?

She didn't think so. In her head she could hear the screaming. Carter.

He'd got under her skin—in every way possible. She'd never felt so connected. So alive. She'd never thought she'd meet anyone she'd consider to be her perfect mate. Even from childhood, she always assumed she'd just meet a guy, get married and have kids. There had been no love hearts and flowers around it. And as she'd got older her view hadn't changed. She'd hoped to meet someone she could be happy with and settle down.

She wasn't even sure she'd believed in love. Until now.

What would happen if she told him that, deep down, she didn't feel she could do this? She didn't feel as though she could stand in a courtroom and try and take a baby from its mother? Would that be it? Her chance at happiness wiped out in one sentence?

The very thought sent a fist closing around her heart and squeezing tight. She couldn't bear that. She couldn't bear the thought of losing him over this. She couldn't bear the thought of going back to her own flat and sleeping in her own bed, alone. She couldn't imagine not seeing Carter every day. She couldn't imagine him not being part of her life.

So what would she have to do to make that happen?

A horrible feeling of dread crept over her. She knew exactly what she had to do. She had to stand in a courtroom, dressed in a business suit, with respectable shirt, shoes and hairstyle, and smile sweetly. She had to expose her life and her sister's to the piranha-like attorney and persuade them that she hadn't donated eggs for the money.

Then she would have to say that she would support Carter in raising this child. This child that she felt no connection with. This child that she felt was someone else's.

The thoughts made her stomach clench. Even though she didn't mean it, even though she didn't really believe it, could she do it?

How much of a sacrifice would it be to stand next to Carter in court and hold his hand? Maybe he wouldn't get full custody of his child—maybe he would have to share custody with Olivia Simpson. Would that really be so bad? Would it be so difficult to help Carter a few days a week with his child? She liked kids, she'd always liked kids, so surely she could manage that?

The trickle of dread was growing, as if ice were circulating around her veins. Her heart was tugging at her, telling her she wasn't really compromising herself, that she was helping the man she loved, the man she wanted to have a future with. Her heart was clamouring so loudly she couldn't hear her head. She couldn't listen to the cold, rational voice that was telling her no man who loved her would ever ask her to do those things. No man

who loved her would expect her to compromise her beliefs and judgement for him.

She walked back over to the desk, staring at the red
folder Rhonda Fulton had left lying there. There was
nothing in that folder she didn't know. There was nothing in that folder that would change how she felt, regardless of the state of her eggs, regardless of the chances of
success of creating embryos and successfully implant-
ing them. She'd told Carter she needed to find out before she could decide.

But it hadn't been true. She'd been stalling for time.
If Rhonda Fulton had told her her eggs had been mislabelled and lost, she'd still be feeling like this. She'd still
be struggling to rationalise the thoughts currently circulating around her head. She'd still be trying to con-
vince herself that helping Carter would be okay. Loving
someone was reason enough to do this.

Rhonda Fulton appeared almost silently, putting a
cup and saucer on the table. She touched Lily's elbow
again. 'Ms Grayson—Lily—I need to go and deal with
one of our patients.' She nodded to the steaming cup of
coffee. 'Please, take your time. If you want to speak to
me again before you go, let my secretary know and she'll
come and find me.' She gave Lily a sympathetic smile
and headed back out the door.

Lily took a sip of the hot coffee, almost feeling the
shot of freshly ground caffeine hit her between the eyes.
This couldn't be the healthy caffeine-free coffee they
normally gave to patients. This must be solely reserved
for staff. And she needed it.

It suddenly struck Lily that not once in their conversation had Rhonda referred to the ongoing court case.
She hadn't mentioned Olivia Simpson or Carter. She
hadn't made reference to the role Lily could play in the

upcoming court case—or how damaging it could be to her clinic. She'd treated Lily professionally and respectfully. She'd treated Lily like the patient she was, not the potential troublemaker she could be. Lily gave a sigh. Maybe she was just being too emotional about all this.

She stood up, straightening her wide-legged trousers and tunic top. At least the walking cast had made her wardrobe more manageable. She was sick of wearing skirts and shapeless jogging pants.

She picked up her bag and folder. It was time to go. She didn't need to speak to Rhonda again. She needed to get out of there. Maybe fresh air would make her feel better? Maybe some sea breezes would salve her conscience about the decision she was about to make, and blow away her troubles in the wind.

She pushed open the door of Rhonda's office and headed back down the corridor. She passed a waiting room filled with patients—the clinic was obviously busy today—headed out the front door and hailed a cab. With her walking cast on she was finally a bit more mobile and could get around more easily. She'd arranged to meet one of her friends—a nurse who was expecting—after her antenatal appointment.

Lily climbed out the cab near the clinic where she was to meet her friend and turned the corner, heading towards the main door, and stopped in her tracks.

Olivia Simpson.

Lily reeled in shock and flattened herself back against the wall of the building. Olivia Simpson was at this clinic. Lily felt her heart thump against her chest. She recognised her immediately. Her picture had been in the newspaper. It had obviously been a picture from a few years ago, but the image had been embedded in her brain.

There was no mistaking her. Lily peeked back around

the corner. Olivia was talking to a man. Tall and handsome with his hand on her shoulder. She pressed back again. They were standing right at the entrance. Lily had arranged to meet her friend inside and this was the only way into the clinic. There was no way Lily was walking past them. If she recognised Olivia from the press pictures, there was every chance that Olivia would recognise her too. Lily cringed—even with her clothes on.

She couldn't even bear to think about what Olivia might say to her. She definitely couldn't bear to see the hurt in her eyes—her body was breaking out into a cold sweat at the mere thought of it. She might normally be feisty and outspoken but nothing about this situation was normal. And the thought of exchanging words with the heavily pregnant woman seemed completely inappropriate.

Lily stood for a few minutes with her heart still thumping in her chest. Maybe if she waited, Olivia would vanish into the crowds on the San Francisco streets.

But curiosity was getting the better of her. This was the woman she would potentially see in court. This was the woman who was carrying Carter's baby.

She stuck her head around the corner carefully. Her breath caught in her throat.

Now she'd got over the shock of seeing her, reality was hitting home. There was no getting away from it. Olivia Simpson looked awful. Her hands were resting on her baby bump and she was talking at length to the man. He was obviously trying to comfort her.

The picture in the newspaper had shown a beautiful blonde-haired, fresh-faced woman. The kind that always drew a second glance. It hadn't been a professional picture—no carefully applied make-up or coiffured hair. It had been a simple snap that had captured the woman's happy expression and natural beauty.

If it hadn't been so engrained in Lily's mind, she would never have recognised her now.

Olivia's hair was straggly. Her skin was pale, almost translucent, with heavy, dark circles under her eyes. There were deep lines in her forehead and around her eyes. And now her hands were moving from her abdomen, twiddling with her hair and being wrung together, over and over again.

But more than all that, for a pregnant woman she looked thin. Her abdomen protruded the way it should, but her face, arms and legs looked gaunt. She looked stressed up to her eyeballs. She looked as if she hadn't slept in weeks. She looked haunted.

She looked as if something could happen to her, or her baby, at any minute.

As a nurse, Lily had always had good instincts. Even when patients were stable, their heart rates and blood pressure entirely normal, Lily had always known when a patient would crash. It was like a sixth sense. One she didn't always welcome. Particularly not now.

Lily felt her legs tremble beneath her, unable to hold her weight. The full emphasis of what she was doing hitting her.

She'd almost decided. She almost decided in that office that she would do it. Her love for Carter superseded her own fundamental beliefs and morals. How could she have let that happen? What kind of a person was she?

Looking at Olivia was all the proof she needed that the doubts and fears she'd had in her mind had been real.

Even when she looked at Olivia's baby bump she felt no connection—no right of parenthood. Because though the baby might be hers in a biological sense, every part of her body was telling her that the baby belonged to Olivia.

She shook her head, trying to control her breathing and bring her racing heart under control. The voices in her head were screaming at her. She couldn't do this. She could never do this. No matter how much she loved Carter. No matter how much she wanted to have a happy-ever-after with him.

It wasn't worth it. For the sake of this woman and her child, it definitely wasn't worth it.

And all of a sudden she felt ashamed. And appalled. Ashamed and appalled that even for a few seconds she'd contemplated doing this because she loved Carter. There was something so wrong about all of this.

He wanted to be a father. He wanted to have a family. This baby was biologically his, he had rights. And while she could understand it, she didn't want to play any part in it.

And if Carter could see Olivia now he would be horrified.

Even looking now, even the slightest glance at that woman and Lily knew she could never do this. Her arms and legs were trembling, tears splashing down her face.

Maybe there was something wrong with her? Maybe she was a hideous person who should never have children—who didn't deserve them? Because no matter how many times she was told that Olivia Simpson was carrying her egg, her baby, she didn't feel the connection. This baby didn't feel like hers in any way, shape or form.

The only reason she'd even contemplated the decision was because of Carter. Because this would give her a permanent connection to Carter.

How sad. How pathetic. How desperate.

She pulled a tissue from her bag and wiped her face,

steadying her legs and sliding back up the wall. She'd made her decision.

She looked round the corner again. Olivia Simpson was gone—the exit was clear. She walked forward, sending a quick text of apology to her friend, and hailed another cab. She knew exactly what she needed to do.

She gave Carter's address to the cab driver and settled back against the cool leather seat.

Maybe love wasn't such a good thing after all? Lots of people said that the first of flush of love generally faded. If she waited long enough, hers would fade too. She had to get some control back.

For the first time in her adult life she'd felt as if she wasn't in control. Lily hated that feeling. She made up her own mind. She didn't allow other people to influence her decisions.

The last time she'd felt out of control had been when she'd been a teenager and her sister had been so ill. The experience had been so traumatic she'd vowed never to let things get like that again.

And all of a sudden she'd nearly been back there. Things spiralling out of control around her, influencing her behaviour, compromising the decisions she made. All because she couldn't get the picture of this man out of her head. All because she would do anything to make him happy.

Her internal autopilot switched on. Her own control mechanism, when things got too hard, that allowed her to function without thinking, switching off her emotional responses.

She could do this. She had to do this.

Her phone sounded. Message from the dark side. She flinched. Sometimes she wondered if he could read her thoughts. Her hands were shaking as she pulled the phone from her bag. Everything ok? C x.

The surge almost overwhelmed her. But she had to be strong. She couldn't let her heart rule her head. Not when the consequences could be so devastating.

The cab journey seemed to pass by in a flash and a few moments later she was standing outside Carter's house again, staring up the long driveway.

She wanted to be here. More than anything she wanted to be here. But she couldn't stay—it just wasn't possible.

She walked around the house, pushing her clothes into a bag, trying to remove all traces of her presence. But it was impossible and she knew it. She picked up the phone and arranged for a company to pick up her bike in the next hour. If only she could ride it home herself. If only she could take off into the hills on her Ducati, the way she normally did, to shake off all her worries and anxieties.

But nothing was going to rid her of this heavy feeling in her heart. Or the permanent lump in her throat.

She stared at the cast around her foot. No matter how uncomfortable and inconvenient it had been, in one way she treasured it. It had brought her and Carter together. It had let her learn to love someone. Something she didn't think she could ever do again.

She positioned herself at the kitchen counter, pad and pen in front of her. How did she write this? How did she explain that her heart was breaking and although she loved him more than she could say, she couldn't give him the one thing he really wanted. His child.

She had to do it like this. She couldn't face seeing him again. One look from those big blue eyes, one touch of his hand on her skin and she would be lost.

It took an hour to finally persuade her that words

would never suffice. The company had picked up her bike and a cab was waiting outside to take her home. She looked around one last time and headed to the door, keying the message into her phone and pressing send.

I'm sorry. L x.

CHAPTER TEN

SOMETHING was wrong. Something didn't feel right. For the first time in his life Carter couldn't concentrate at work. Normally he was focused, on the ball and never distracted. Today he was useless. And the lack of sleep last night hadn't helped.

He stared at the computer screen in front of him. He was supposed to be checking the theatre lists and the patients his secretary had scheduled for surgery. It was just as well she was good at her job, as he couldn't focus.

Cole had been on the phone again this morning, discussing his plan. And his plan had made Carter's blood run cold. The man was only doing his job, he was doing his absolute best to ensure Carter won custody of his baby. But his methods were questionable. After several false starts he was going after Olivia Simpson and the fact she might be pursuing a relationship with another man.

If Carter had been in a different state of mind he might have been angry. He might have been annoyed and wondered how she could even think of pursuing a relationship at this time. But the truth was, he couldn't summon up any of those emotions. Olivia was a widow, thrust into a dreadful set of circumstances.

He, more than anyone, knew that sometimes, even at the most inopportune moment, you could meet someone and things just clicked. He knew how people could be unexpectedly thrust together. It was the same set of circumstances for him and Lily, so how could he stand in judgement of someone who'd done the same thing he had?

The serious doubts that were already circulating in his mind were starting to gather a momentum of their own.

He pulled his phone from his pocket again. He'd been on call last night and had spent all night in Theatre after a nasty RTA. He'd sent texts to Lily last night and this morning and she hadn't replied. Was she all right? How had she got on at the clinic yesterday? Were her eggs safe?

All of a sudden the potential horrors of an IVF clinic didn't seem like the most important thing any more. He'd done it once. He could do it again—if that's what she wanted.

Because as much as Carter wanted kids, he couldn't imagine doing it without Lily.

Because she was the biggest constant here. She was the immovable object in his plan. None of this mattered without her. Kids or no kids.

His head was spinning. He wanted to talk to her. He wanted to know how she felt. He wanted to know how she felt about him and how she felt about the custody battle.

Lily was the only person who'd asked him the hard questions. She was the only person to question his motives. She'd been the only person to sit him down and make him stop and think. Why was he doing this? Why was it so important to him? Yes, this child was biologically his. But this child was unexpected. And not in the way that some men found out about an unknown child.

These embryos had been created for him and Tabitha to use within their marriage. But their marriage was long since over and Tabitha was nowhere to be found. It was kind of ironic. As if someone up there was trying to send him a message.

Carter let out a stream of air through his pursed lips. These embryos were supposed to have been destroyed—and he'd accepted that. But this whole thing had came like a bolt from the blue, sending waves of emotion and a single-mindedness that had made him act without thinking. He'd been so caught up in the legalities and complexities of the case that he hadn't really stopped to consider the other people involved. Olivia Simpson. Lily Grayson. His child.

And there was another thought circulating around his brain. One that was so shocking he kept trying to push it away. But it was persistent. And it wouldn't let him go.

What if he stopped all this? What if he let Olivia Simpson keep the baby? The mere thought sent a shiver down his spine.

What kind of a person would that make him? What kind of a man walked away from his child?

Everything about that seemed wrong. Everything about that seemed alien to him. But the thought kept clamouring around in his head, along with all his doubts and insecurities about bringing up a baby on his own.

This was never how he would have imagined things. He believed in family. He believed in children being brought up in a family with two parents who loved each other. The irony was, he had lots of friends who were single parents and did a wonderful job. And he was sure, if it came to it, he could do it too.

It was just that in his head that wasn't the way he'd pictured his life. He knew there were good reasons for parents to be on their own, he'd just never imagined it would be him. He always wanted to do this with someone else—someone he loved and could share the journey with.

So why did it feel as if that chance was slipping through his fingers like grains of sand on a beach?

Right now, more than anything, he needed to talk to Lily. He needed to tell her about the feeling deep in the pit of his stomach—the one that was telling him to stop all this now.

He needed to see the look on her face when he told her he'd made up his mind to let his child go.

He needed to know she wasn't disappointed in him. And that if he did this, she'd still be able to love him.

His phone beeped. It must be Lily. He fumbled to pull it out of his pocket and in his haste sent it crashing to the floor.

He screwed up his face. The most technologically advanced phone on the market and the screen was cracked. It would probably cost an arm and a leg to replace it. He touched the screen to reveal the message.

I'm sorry. L x.

What? His heart plummeted. What did that mean? Even through the cracked screen there was no mistaking the message. What had happened?

His fingers pressed dial straight away and he held the phone to his ear. Nothing. It automatically went to voicemail. He stood up from his desk and grabbed his jacket. She must be at home. He'd find her there.

He needed to know what was going on. He needed to know why she was sorry. Was it the case? Had she decided she couldn't appear in court?

Because he could live with that. She didn't want her family history exposed and that was fine. What he couldn't live without was Lily.

He needed her. He needed to be able to wrap his arms around her. He needed to be able to hear her voice, smell her perfume and touch her skin.

Because above all else—he loved her.

Carter gunned his bike and pulled into his driveway a little while later. He tilted his head as he pulled off his helmet. Why was there light shining under the garage door?

He pulled out his key and strode through the house, heading straight to the interlocking door for the garage. He pulled it open.

And stared around at the wide space. Her bike was gone.

His footsteps quickened as he paced through the house to the bedroom. The wardrobe doors lay open, revealing the emptiness inside. The drawers on the dresser were pulled open, as if someone had left in a hurry.

He couldn't believe it. He couldn't believe she would leave without talking to him first. Without telling him why she was going.

No. Scratch that. Let's start at the beginning. He couldn't believe that she'd gone.

After all that they'd shared. How could she leave?

His head went from side to side as he walked through the rest of the house and into the kitchen. He looked for a letter, a note—something, anything—from her. Every trace of her was gone.

Though not entirely. He could still smell her scent, her light honeysuckle perfume still floating through the air towards him.

Carter could feel panic creep through his veins, a sensation completely unfamiliar to him. He never panicked. He was always calm in crisis. He could always keep his head.

So why did all rational thought leave when it came to Lily?

He hit redial on his phone. He called her mobile and the number for her house. Still no answer. Where was she?

He leaned back against the kitchen counter. She'd moved her bike from his garage. She couldn't have done that herself—she still had a cast on. She must have needed some help. He walked towards the phone, finding the telephone directory lying open next to it. There! A tiny pencil mark above one of the company names, as if she'd poised above it while phoning. He dialled quickly. 'Hi, it's John Carter. You picked up a bike from my address for a Lily Grayson...' He reeled off his address. 'Can I just confirm that it's arrived at the delivery address?'

He held his breath, praying the man at the other end of the phone wouldn't think twice. He was lucky.

'It'll be at Tennison Street tomorrow morning. It was too busy to do a drop-off in the rush-hour. We've left a message for Ms Grayson.'

Carter hung up, breathing sigh of relief. She'd gone home. If she'd gone elsewhere he would have had no idea how to find her.

His heartbeat started to quicken. He could do this. He could find her and tell her his decision.

He strode back to the front door. Five minutes after he'd arrived, he was ready to leave again. Almost.

'Woah!'

Both men shouted simultaneously, Carter from the shock of seeing someone on his doorstep as he nearly crashed into them and the UPS driver as the door he was about to knock on flew open.

The UPS driver recovered quickest, handing Carter his electronic signature keypad. 'John Carter? I need you to sign for a delivery.'

Carter scribbled his nondescript signature and grabbed the proffered envelope. He didn't have time for this right now. He had to find Lily.

Until he caught sight of the name and return address on the envelope. Olivia Simpson. Hillsborough.

His head shot upwards. She lived right here. She lived somewhere close by. And he'd never known it.

Why on earth was she sending him a letter? He'd never tried to contact her at all. Everything had been done via Cole.

Was this really from Olivia—or was it from her attorney?

Then his eyes captured the date. Nearly two weeks ago. The UPS guy was already halfway down the path.

'Hold on a minute.' Carter jogged down the path after him.

The guy was already looking at his electronic keypad, concentrating on his next delivery.

'That date,' Carter said quickly. 'This was posted nearly two weeks ago.'

The delivery man squinted at the date and pulled up something on his screen. 'Oh, yeah. Sorry about that. We had a problem with one of our trucks. It went off the road after an accident and we didn't realise there were some deliveries still wedged behind the driver's seat.' He gave Carter a half-hearted smile. 'Sorry about that. It's never happened before.' He shrugged his shoulders and headed back to his van.

Carter stared at the letter in his hand. His front door was lying open and he heard the phone start to ring inside. The thought was instant. Lily! It could be Lily.

He ran back inside and snatched the phone up. 'Lily?'

'Carter? Carter, it's Cole. There's some news. You're a father. You've got a baby boy. Congratulations.'

All at once the world came crashing down around his ears.

He was a mess. He didn't know what to do next. He didn't know if was allowed to go and see his son or not. He didn't know which hospital his thirty-four-week-old baby was in. He had to wait for Cole to contact him again.

And more than anything, right now he really needed to speak to Lily. He needed to hear her voice. He wanted to hold her hand. He needed her by his side.

His fingers tightened around the thin envelope. Part of him didn't want to open it. Life was complicated enough. He had enough voices currently clamouring in his head without letting Olivia Simpson's in there too.

But the voice that was loudest surprised him. It was his mother's. Telling him to be calm, asking him what had happened to his common sense. Asking him why he hadn't sat down and spoken to this woman.

But this was America—and you didn't do that in America any more. Everyone hired attorneys. For everything.

Give her a fair hearing. Will she get it in court?

His mother's voice echoed again, banishing all the final doubts from his mind. He could see her in his head. Her tall, slim figure and pale grey eyes. No degree, no university education, but probably the wisest woman he had ever known. The wisdom of the world had been written on her face.

A smile crossed his face. For the first time ever he realised something—without a shadow of a doubt. She would have loved Lily.

Almost automatically he tore the envelope open, pulled out the letter and started reading.

It was a handwritten letter from Olivia. Written two weeks ago when she must have learned that Carter intended to fight for custody of his child. His mind tried to work out the dates. She'd written this after it had been touch and go with the baby and the in utero blood transfusion had taken place. The writing was shaky in places and smudged—from tears?

Carter sat down and read. And read. And read.

It was everything he could have wanted and more. Relief swept through him. Olivia Simpson was reaffirming everything that he'd considered in the last few days. He was making the right decision—he just had to tell Lily.

Lily was sitting in her darkened flat when the loud rap at the door sounded. She jumped. She'd been there so long night had fallen across the city and she hadn't even turned on a light.

She gazed at the mounds of sodden tissues on the sofa next to her—she'd run out so had started to use her sleeve. Lovely.

'Lily, let me in.' The knock was louder this time.

Her chest tightened. Carter. She'd known it would be him. She'd known he wouldn't let her walk away like that. She walked over to the mirror. She looked a fright. Her mascara had run down her face in black streams and her hair was sticking up like a haystack.

She walked over to the door and peered through the peephole.

Bad idea. Carter. Dressed in his leathers, helmet in hand, looking very frustrated, pacing up and down. Even the sight of him made her heart lurch. The broad shoulders, muscled chest and tight buttocks. She wanted to open the door and collapse into his arms.

But she didn't want him to see her like this. All bleary-eyed and blotchy. One touch from him and all her resolve would be out the window.

She leaned against the door. She wasn't strong enough to open it. 'What do you want, Carter?' She tried to hide the tremble in her voice, she had to be strong.

He must have heard her because seconds later his voice came through the apartment door to her. 'Open the door, Lily. Please.'

The tears automatically welled in her eyes again. 'I can't.' She pressed her head against the door. 'Please don't do this. It's already too hard.'

'Lily, please. I need to speak to you.' There was silence for a few moments, he was obviously trying to give her some time. It was no use. She wanted to see him, she wanted to speak to him. At the very least she wanted the opportunity to say goodbye to the man she could have loved for ever.

But for a second her mind was full of what-ifs? What if there was a way to make this work? What if he felt the same way about her as she did about him? What if there was even a tiny chance of future together? Her hands were shaking as she lifted them to the lock.

'I have a son.'

Her hands and stomach dropped simultaneously. She felt sick. She felt physically sick. This was it. It was over.

That's why Carter was here.

He had his son now. And he wanted custody. This wasn't about her. This wasn't about them. He was here to persuade her to help him in court. She felt as if he'd just twisted a knife through her heart.

She couldn't speak. Her feet felt as though they were made of lead. She couldn't move. So much for what-ifs?

His voice came through the door again, whispering through the seam of the door—as if he knew her ear was pressed there.

'I need you, Lily.'

It was the words she wanted to hear. But not in these circumstances. Not like this. Not when he didn't mean them. A single fat tear slid down her cheek.

His voice continued. 'I love you, Lily. I haven't said those words before but I want you to know that's how I feel. I know the timing is terrible, but I can't change how I feel and I don't want to.'

She was frozen in place, hypnotised by his voice.

'You're the first thing I think about in the morning and the last thing I think about at night. You're the person I want to create a future with. You're the person I want to have a family with—I want to have a house full of little Carters and Lilys. But even if that never happens—even if we can't have children together—I can't imagine my future without you. I don't want to have a future without you in it.'

She wanted to believe all this—she wanted to believe

it was true and that he felt the same way about her as she did about him. He was creating images in her head that were breaking her heart. 'I can't do it,' she whispered. 'I can't help you.' She curled her head down towards her chest.

'I don't want you to help me.'

'What?' Her head shot back upwards and she faced the door, standing on tiptoe and peering back through the peephole. Her heart was thudding in her chest. What did he mean?

He was standing directly in front of the door, holding a crumpled piece of paper in his hand, holding it up as if he knew she was looking at him.

For the first time she studied his face, noticing his bloodshot eyes. Had Carter been crying? Had something happened to the baby?

She didn't stop to think any further. Her hands flew to the lock and she jerked the door open. 'What is it?' Her voice was breathless as her chest constricted. He was inches away from her. Inches away from her touch.

She could just reach out and put her hands on his broad chest, slide them around his waist and onto his tight buttocks. She could pull him close to her.

'I got a letter from Olivia. She asked me not to pursue custody of the baby. The only thing is—she wrote this letter two weeks ago.' He hadn't even finished talking before Lily had pulled the proffered letter from his hand and started reading. Her eyes skimmed the page frantically. If she'd thought she'd been crying before, it was nothing compared to now.

This was a letter pleading from the heart. Someone who loved her baby with her whole heart and soul. Someone who would die for her baby. The genetics didn't matter to her. From the second that little child had started to grow inside her she'd loved it for all the right reasons.

She was terrified. She was terrified of the medical complications her child was facing. She'd already thought she might lose the baby that way, but to get through that and now face this? The thought of losing her baby another way was too much for her.

Lily sagged back against the doorframe. Her head was spinning. She frowned at him. 'How long have you had this, Carter?' The thought that he'd had this woman's letter for two weeks and not responded was unimaginable. The thought he hadn't told her was even worse. Her head started shaking at the very thought of it. He wasn't that kind of man. She knew he wasn't that kind of man.

'I got it this afternoon. It's been stuck in a delivery truck for two weeks.'

'Oh, Carter. What are you going to do?' She could almost feel Olivia's pain in her chest. Her eyes searched his face for a clue to what he might be thinking. She had to tell him. She had to tell him why she couldn't help him. This letter reinforced all the fears and doubts that had been circulating in her head for the last few weeks.

'I saw her.'

'What?'

'Yesterday. I saw her outside one of the antenatal clinics. I went to meet one my friends and she was standing outside with a man. She looked awful, Carter, and as soon as I saw her I knew I couldn't help you. Everything about it seemed wrong. The thought of Cole cross-examining her in court, delving into her private life and picking her apart. I just couldn't do it—no matter how I feel about you. I'm so sorry.'

Something flitted across his face. Was it anger? It was something she didn't recognise, something she couldn't place. The deep frown lines on his forehead relaxed. There was still sadness in his eyes, but there was definitely something else. Was it relief?

He touched her hand, sending a pulse of electric currents up her arm. 'How do you feel about me, Lily?'

She gulped. A direct question with him staring straight into her eyes. For so many reasons she wanted to lie right now. She wanted to tell him he didn't matter to her—it had just been a fling. It would be best. Then he could walk away without giving her a thought. But she couldn't. She couldn't lie to him.

'I love you, Carter. I think I'm always going to love you,' she whispered.

He nodded slowly and took a deep breath. 'Then I need you beside me. For ever. Because I can't do this, Lily. I can't do this either. I'd already made up my mind before the letter arrived. I can't take my child away from his mother. No matter how I feel about all this, my son has a right to be loved and cared for by his mother. I can't deny him that.'

'What?' She didn't understand. She'd thought he was there to persuade her to help him in court. She'd thought he'd be angry with her. This was the last thing she'd expected.

'Because of this letter?'

'No...and yes. This letter helps. It tells me I'm doing the right thing. But I'd already made up my mind. I was coming to tell you—to talk to you about this—when the delivery man arrived. This is about us, about you and me.'

'No, Carter.' She couldn't bear this. She couldn't bear

the thought that he might walk away from his child because of her. It was a recipe for disaster. He would grow to hate her, resent her, and she couldn't live with that.

'Don't do this for me, Carter. I don't want you to do this for me.' She pressed her hand around his arm. 'Have you thought about this? Have you really thought about this? What if you walk away now and that's it? What if you never have the chance to have children and you've walked away from the only biological child you will ever have? Have you thought about that?'

She knew she sounded desperate—but she was. Her mind was filled with rosy pictures of Carter's back yard filled with a gaggle of children but that might never happen. She wanted Carter to have his happy-ever-after—even if that was never with her. He deserved it. And because she loved him she wanted him to have it.

He walked up to her, his frame looming over hers. She could see the shadow of bristles on his chin, the tiny bloodshot vessels in his eyes. He had been crying. His hands rested on her shoulders and his fingers started entwining themselves through her hair. She tilted her head towards them, her natural response. She wanted to feel his touch, she wanted to feel his skin against hers.

One finger started to stroke the side of her cheek, tracing a line across her eyebrows and the bridge of her nose. 'I have thought about it.' His voice was calm and determined. 'It's all I've thought about for the last four weeks. But I've been having doubts. And I hated myself for them.' He touched the letter in her hand. 'But this just made all the pieces of the jigsaw puzzle fall into place. Biology doesn't make a child. Biology doesn't make a parent.' He laid his hand on her chest. 'It's what's in here that counts.'

She could feel the warmth of his palm spreading through her skin. She was sure he must feel her heartbeat quickening at his touch. His voice was husky. 'Olivia is the true parent of this child. And I need to let her be.'

Lily felt dizzy. Her legs felt weak, as if they couldn't hold her weight. Was he really going to do this?

Her voice was shaking. 'You're really not going to take her to court?' She lifted her hands and pressed them on his chest. She needed to feel him. She needed to feel the warmth of his body under her palms.

He stared at her with those big deep eyes. 'I'm really not going to take her court.'

'But what about the future?'

'I hope that Olivia will let me have some contact, some news about my son. I'd like to know that he's healthy and well. This is uncharted territory for me.' He cupped his hand behind her head, pulling her closer to him. 'But my future is with you. Whatever that may be. I just want a chance to find out. I want to see you every morning when I wake up.' His face carved into a smile. 'I want to watch you wreck every piece of equipment in my house. I want to go on bike rides with you into the Napa Valley. I want to do parachute jumps together but most of all I want to grow old with you and have matching rocking chairs on the porch.'

A smile broke out across her face. The tears were still flowing but these were happy tears, not sad ones. Tears of joy and tears of relief.

'You've no idea how much I've wanted you to say all that.'

'So what do you say, Lily? Will you come home with me?'

She didn't hesitate, even for a fraction of a second.

Because this was her happy-every-after with the man she loved. Whatever happened with Olivia and the baby they'd work it out together. Because that's what you did with someone you loved.

He picked up the phone.

'What are you doing?'

His arm tightened around her waist, drawing her closer to him as his lips brushed against hers. 'I'm changing the delivery address for your bike. I'm getting them to take it back home.'

'Home.' She wound her arms around his neck as the warm feeling spread through her body. 'That sounds good.'

And she rose up on tiptoe and kissed him.

* * * * *

Mills & Boon® Hardback
September 2012

ROMANCE

Unlocking her Innocence	Lynne Graham
Santiago's Command	Kim Lawrence
His Reputation Precedes Him	Carole Mortimer
The Price of Retribution	Sara Craven
Just One Last Night	Helen Brooks
The Greek's Acquisition	Chantelle Shaw
The Husband She Never Knew	Kate Hewitt
When Only Diamonds Will Do	Lindsay Armstrong
The Couple Behind the Headlines	Lucy King
The Best Mistake of Her Life	Aimee Carson
The Valtieri Baby	Caroline Anderson
Slow Dance with the Sheriff	Nikki Logan
Bella's Impossible Boss	Michelle Douglas
The Tycoon's Secret Daughter	Susan Meier
She's So Over Him	Joss Wood
Return of the Last McKenna	Shirley Jump
Once a Playboy…	Kate Hardy
Challenging the Nurse's Rules	Janice Lynn

MEDICAL

Her Motherhood Wish	Anne Fraser
A Bond Between Strangers	Scarlet Wilson
The Sheikh and the Surrogate Mum	Meredith Webber
Tamed by her Brooding Boss	Joanna Neil

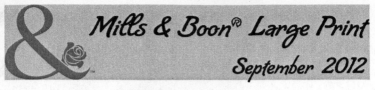

Mills & Boon® Large Print

September 2012

ROMANCE

A Vow of Obligation	Lynne Graham
Defying Drakon	Carole Mortimer
Playing the Greek's Game	Sharon Kendrick
One Night in Paradise	Maisey Yates
Valtieri's Bride	Caroline Anderson
The Nanny Who Kissed Her Boss	Barbara McMahon
Falling for Mr Mysterious	Barbara Hannay
The Last Woman He'd Ever Date	Liz Fielding
His Majesty's Mistake	Jane Porter
Duty and the Beast	Trish Morey
The Darkest of Secrets	Kate Hewitt

HISTORICAL

Lady Priscilla's Shameful Secret	Christine Merrill
Rake with a Frozen Heart	Marguerite Kaye
Miss Cameron's Fall from Grace	Helen Dickson
Society's Most Scandalous Rake	Isabelle Goddard
The Taming of the Rogue	Amanda McCabe

MEDICAL

Falling for the Sheikh She Shouldn't	Fiona McArthur
Dr Cinderella's Midnight Fling	Kate Hardy
Brought Together by Baby	Margaret McDonagh
One Month to Become a Mum	Louisa George
Sydney Harbour Hospital: Luca's Bad Girl	Amy Andrews
The Firebrand Who Unlocked His Heart	Anne Fraser

0812 GEN STD LP

ROMANCE

Banished to the Harem	Carol Marinelli
Not Just the Greek's Wife	Lucy Monroe
A Delicious Deception	Elizabeth Power
Painted the Other Woman	Julia James
A Game of Vows	Maisey Yates
A Devil in Disguise	Caitlin Crews
Revelations of the Night Before	Lynn Raye Harris
Defying her Desert Duty	Annie West
The Wedding Must Go On	Robyn Grady
The Devil and the Deep	Amy Andrews
Taming the Brooding Cattleman	Marion Lennox
The Rancher's Unexpected Family	Myrna Mackenzie
Single Dad's Holiday Wedding	Patricia Thayer
Nanny for the Millionaire's Twins	Susan Meier
Truth-Or-Date.com	Nina Harrington
Wedding Date with Mr Wrong	Nicola Marsh
The Family Who Made Him Whole	Jennifer Taylor
The Doctor Meets Her Match	Annie Claydon

MEDICAL

A Socialite's Christmas Wish	Lucy Clark
Redeeming Dr Riccardi	Leah Martyn
The Doctor's Lost-and-Found Heart	Dianne Drake
The Man Who Wouldn't Marry	Tina Beckett

0912 GEN STD HB

ROMANCE

A Secret Disgrace	Penny Jordan
The Dark Side of Desire	Julia James
The Forbidden Ferrara	Sarah Morgan
The Truth Behind his Touch	Cathy Williams
Plain Jane in the Spotlight	Lucy Gordon
Battle for the Soldier's Heart	Cara Colter
The Navy SEAL's Bride	Soraya Lane
My Greek Island Fling	Nina Harrington
Enemies at the Altar	Melanie Milburne
In the Italian's Sights	Helen Brooks
In Defiance of Duty	Caitlin Crews

HISTORICAL

The Duchess Hunt	Elizabeth Beacon
Marriage of Mercy	Carla Kelly
Unbuttoning Miss Hardwick	Deb Marlowe
Chained to the Barbarian	Carol Townend
My Fair Concubine	Jeannie Lin

MEDICAL

Georgie's Big Greek Wedding?	Emily Forbes
The Nurse's Not-So-Secret Scandal	Wendy S. Marcus
Dr Right All Along	Joanna Neil
Summer With A French Surgeon	Margaret Barker
Sydney Harbour Hospital: Tom's Redemption	Fiona Lowe
Doctor on Her Doorstep	Annie Claydon